"Do you think he could have been the one—" her throat moved as she swallowed convulsively, probably choking on nerves or fear "—that put me in the trunk?"

Dalton reached for her, sliding his arm around her shoulders to offer her comfort. She trembled against him, and he tightened his embrace. "Of course not," he said. "I wouldn't have brought you along if I thought he could be the one who had hurt you."

She had thought that all this time and had been willing to confront her attacker? He'd known she was strong, but her fearlessness overwhelmed him.

Instead of cowering, she opened her door and stepped out to confront her fear or her elusive memories. Dalton jumped out the driver's-side door and hurried around to her side of the car. They hadn't been followed. But if the killer had figured out that they might come back here...

He didn't want her far from his side in the dimly lit parking garage. He didn't want to lose her.

AGENT TO THE RESCUE

LISA CHILDS

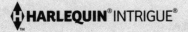

With great pride and appreciation for my daughters, Ashley & Chloe Theeuwes— for being such strong, smart young women!

ISBN-13: 978-0-373-74913-3

Agent to the Rescue

Copyright © 2015 by Lisa Childs

Recycling programs for this product may not exist in your area.

Printed in U.S.A.

HARLEQUIN®

www.Harlequin.com

Lisa Childs writes paranormal and contemporary romance for Harlequin. She lives on thirty acres in Michigan with her two daughters, a talkative Siamese and a long-haired Chihuahua who thinks she's a rottweiler. Lisa loves hearing from readers, who can contact her through her website, lisachilds.com, or snail-mail address, PO Box 139, Marne, MI 49435.

Books by Lisa Childs

Harlequin Intrigue

Special Agents at the Altar

The Pregnant Witness
Agent Undercover
Agent to the Rescue

Shotgun Weddings

Groom Under Fire
Explosive Engagement
Bridegroom Bodyguard

Visit the Author Profile page at Harlequin.com for more titles.

CAST OF CHARACTERS

Special Agent Dalton Reyes—The FBI agent grew up in a gang and works the organized crime division of the Bureau, so he's out of his element when he finds a bride in the trunk of a car. She brings out a protective side of him that has him risking his life for hers.

Jane Doe aka Elizabeth Schroeder—She has no idea how she wound up in the trunk of a car in a wedding dress and veil. She has no idea who she even is, but she knows she's in danger and can only trust one man—Dalton Reyes.

Trooper Littlefield—The state trooper tipped off Reyes about the car, but he has a connection to the bride that he hasn't revealed.

Special Agent Jared Bell—The FBI profiler is obsessed with the serial killer who's eluded him for years—the one who kills brides. He thinks Jane Doe would have been his next victim if not for Dalton saving her.

Tom Wilson—The handsome lawyer never reported his fiancée as missing—maybe because he didn't want her body found.

Patricia Cunningham—Elizabeth's friend was also a victim, but she didn't survive the attempt on her life.

Kenneth Cunningham—Patricia's husband took her life and then his own. But Elizabeth, convinced they were both murdered, wants the investigation reopened. Her determination might be why someone wants her dead, too.

Lizzie Cunningham—The two-year-old already lost her parents. Elizabeth and Dalton need to keep her safe and make sure she doesn't lose anyone else in her life.

Gregory Cunningham—Kenneth's brother isn't surprised by how his brother and sister-in-law died, but he is surprised that they named Elizabeth his niece's guardian instead of him.

Ronnie Hoover—The ex-con is determined to never return to jail, so he can't risk getting caught…

Chapter One

The noose tightening around his neck, Dalton Reyes struggled to swallow even his own saliva. His mouth was dry, though, because fear and nerves overwhelmed him. He tugged at the too-tight bow tie and thanked God he wasn't the one getting married right now.

He couldn't imagine promising to love one woman for the rest of his life and then to spend the rest of his life trying to make that one woman happy. Even though he didn't want that for himself, Dalton stood at Ash Stryker's side as the FBI special agent vowed just that to Claire Molenski.

Ash turned and looked at him, his blue eyes narrowed in a warning glare. Realizing he'd missed his cue, Dalton hurriedly reached into his pocket for the ring. Why the hell had he wanted to be the best man? Wearing the monkey suit was bad enough, but having to keep track of the damn ring, too…

It was too much. He would rather have mobsters shooting at him than this pressure of the whole church watching him. At least the church was small. But it was hot and stuffy, too. Sweat beaded on his lip, but then his fingers encountered the band. And he pulled out the delicate gold ring. It was tiny—just like the bride.

The first time he had met Claire Molenski, he'd thought the little blonde was hot. But she looked like something else in that white gown—like an angel. Dalton had always preferred bad girls, the ones who wore too much makeup and too-little leather skirts.

As soon as the ceremony was over, he rushed outside and gulped some air.

"You'd think you were the groom," a man teased him from the shadows of a huge oak. "With as much as you were sweating up there…"

"That'll never happen," Dalton replied with the confidence of a man who had never been in love and never intended to take that fall. "I won't ever be anyone's groom."

Finally the man stepped from the shadows. He'd beaten Dalton outside, so he must have been there before the ceremony had even ended. Apparently, though, he had been inside the church long enough to see Dalton sweating at the altar. Since he'd left early, he didn't seem to like weddings any more than Dalton did.

Then Dalton recognized him and realized why. "You're Jared Bell…"

The man was a legendary FBI profiler. Recruited out of college into the Bureau, he already had a long and illustrious career for his young age. But he was almost more legendary for the serial killer he hadn't caught than for all those that he had. The sick bastard who'd eluded him had had a thing for killing brides….

It probably hadn't been easy for him to see Claire in that white dress and not imagine all those other brides who hadn't lived long enough to wed their grooms. All those victims…

Jared Bell extended his hand to Dalton. "And you're Agent Reyes."

He should have been flattered that the profiler knew him. But then Dalton Reyes wasn't so much legendary as notorious—for growing up in a gang but then leaving the streets to become a cop and then an FBI special agent assigned to the organized crime division.

"Nice to meet you," he said. With a glance back at the church, he asked, "I take it you know Ash…"

The grinning groom stood on the stairs of the stuffy little chapel with his smiling bride clasped tightly against his side. Ash Stryker couldn't take his hands off the petite blonde, but Dalton didn't blame him.

Bell nodded. "Yes, I know Ash. Not as well as you do, apparently, since you were his best man."

Reyes grinned at the surprise in the other man's voice. "You thought it would be Blaine Campbell?"

Bell nodded again. "Stryker and Campbell were marines together."

The two marines had known each other longer than Dalton had known either of them. So he was pretty sure that Blaine Campbell had been Ash's first choice, but somehow *he* had wound up with the honor. Ash and Claire had told him it was because they probably wouldn't have made it to the altar without him. A lot of people had recently been trying really hard to kill them. He had helped out, but he'd only been doing his job.

A job he loved. He still couldn't believe that Ash was cutting back—no longer going undercover. Dalton shook his head and sighed. He had wanted to stand up as best man for Ash, but he didn't agree with him.

His cell rang, saving him from making a reply to Jared Bell. He fished his phone from the pocket of his black tuxedo jacket.

"Good thing it didn't ring in the church," Bell remarked drily.

Dalton nodded in agreement. He probably would have been fired on the spot from his position as best man. He glanced at the screen of the cell phone. Why would the local police-post Dispatch be calling him?

"I have to take this," he said "But I hope we get a chance to talk some more at the reception."

Bell sighed. He probably thought Dalton wanted to talk about what everybody always wanted to talk about—that case that had never been solved.

Dalton clicked on his phone. "Agent Reyes here."

"This is Michigan state trooper Littlefield," a male voice identified himself. "I heard you might be in my area for a wedding."

Littlefield had helped Campbell, Ash and Reyes apprehend some bank robbery suspects at a cottage in a wooded area nearby this chapel. It was how Ash had heard about the wedding venue. And Littlefield must have heard about the wedding because he'd been invited.

"I'm in your neck of the woods," Dalton admitted. "Why aren't you at the wedding?"

"I'm working," Littlefield said. "I couldn't get off duty. I had Dispatch patch me through to your cell. Are you working?"

Harder than he'd thought he would have to as best man. "Not at the moment…"

"What I mean is," the trooper clarified, "are you still working that car theft ring?"

It seemed as if he was always working a car theft ring. He would no sooner shut down one operation before another would spring up. Sometimes he went undercover himself; sometimes he used informants, but he hadn't failed yet to solve a case. This case was giving him trouble, though—probably because the operation was a lot more widespread than he'd originally anticipated.

"Yeah, I'm still working it." He had recently put out a bulletin to state police departments and sheriffs' offices to keep an eye out for any suspicious vehicles.

"I just passed a strange Mercedes heading down a dirt road," Littlefield shared, his voice full of suspicion. "It looked vintage."

A vintage Mercedes on a dirt road? It was unlikely that the car owner would have risked the paint or the suspension of the luxury vehicle.

"Where are you?" Reyes asked. "And how do I get there?"

"Aren't you at a wedding?"

Ash would understand. Maybe.

Dalton had been chasing these car thieves for a while. But he hadn't caught them—probably because their chop shop was off some dirt road in some obscure wooded area.

Like here…

He tugged his bow tie loose as he headed

for his SUV. With its power-charged engine, he should be able to catch up to that Mercedes in no time.

THE BRONZE-COLORED MERCEDES fishtailed along the gravel road, kicking up a cloud of dust, as Dalton pursued it. He had caught up to it in less time than he'd anticipated. Now his anticipation grew. If he could follow it back to the chop shop...

But the driver must have spotted Littlefield's patrol car following at a discreet distance. And the Mercedes had sped up to lose the trooper. The Bureau SUV was more powerful, though, and had easily passed the patrol car. Dalton had caught sight of the Mercedes, but had the driver caught sight of him yet?

Could he see the black SUV through the cloud of dust flying up behind his spinning tires?

Even if he hadn't seen him, the driver wasn't likely to go back to the chop shop now. He was more likely to try to dump the car since a trooper had seen it. Littlefield hadn't gotten close enough to read the plate, though.

Dalton was getting close enough, but too much dirt obscured the numbers and letters. Actually, he couldn't even tell if there was a plate on the car at all. Then the Mercedes accelerated again. The driver must have seen him.

Dalton pressed on his gas pedal, revving the engine. But his tires slid on the loose gravel. The road wasn't driven that often, so it wasn't well maintained. There were deep ruts, and the shoulders of the road had washed out into water-filled gullies on either side. If he lost control, he might wind up in one of those gullies. So he eased off the gas slightly and regained control.

A city kid born and raised, Dalton wasn't used to driving on dirt roads. The driver of the Mercedes had no such problem. Maybe he had grown up around this area, because the car disappeared around a sharp curve in the road.

Dalton cursed. He had been so close. He couldn't lose him now. He sped up and fishtailed around the curve, nearly losing control. The SUV took the corner on two wheels. Worried that he was going to roll the vehicle, he cursed some more. Then the tires dropped back down and the SUV skidded across the road—toward one of those gullies.

He braked hard and gritted his teeth to hold in more curses as the SUV continued its skid. He grasped the wheel hard and steered away from the ditch. Finally he regained control only to fight for it again, around the next curve. He skidded and nearly collided with the rear bumper of the Mercedes; it was the only part of the luxury vehicle that wasn't in the ditch.

Maybe its driver hadn't been as familiar with the roads as Dalton had thought—since he'd gone off in the gully himself. The tires of the SUV squealed as he braked hard again. He shoved the gearshift into Park and hopped out of the driver's side. His weapon drawn from beneath his tuxedo jacket, he slowly approached the vintage Mercedes.

Its engine was still running, smoke trailing up from beneath its crumpled hood. The water in the gully sizzled from the heat of it. The Mercedes wasn't going anywhere now. But the driver was gone—probably out the open passenger's window.

Dalton lifted his gun toward the woods on that side of the road. The driver had disappeared into them. But he could be close, just hiding behind a tree. Or he could be following a trail through those woods to that chop shop Dalton was determined to find. Since he was a city kid, he would probably get lost. But he started down toward the ditch, anyway, to follow the driver into those woods.

Then the smooth soles of his once-shiny black dress shoes slipped on the loose gravel and the muddy bank. He started sliding toward the water—which he wouldn't have minded falling into if the damn tux wasn't an expensive rental. To steady himself, he grabbed at the Mercedes and braced his hand on the trunk. But then his hand slid the way his shoes had. He glanced down and figured out why when he saw the blood on his palm. It was also smeared beneath the dust across the trunk lid.

Dread tightened his stomach into a tight knot. Growing up where he had and working in the division he worked, he had already found more than his share of bodies in car trunks. But he suspected he was about to find another.

He had nothing on him to pry open the lid or to break the lock. So he took the easy way and kicked in the driver's window, which started an alarm blaring. Then he reached inside for the trunk-lid release button. Fortunately the car wasn't so vintage that it hadn't come equipped with some more up-to-date features. The button clicked, and the trunk lid flew up, waving like a flag in the woods.

It wasn't a surrender flag, though, because the driver had fled into the woods and apparently for a damn good reason, too. Even if the car wasn't stolen, he would have had some trouble explaining the body in the trunk.

Sun shone through the trees of the thick woods and glinted off that trunk lid. It was such a beautiful day for a wedding. Dalton should have stayed at the stuffy little church and celebrated with his deservedly happy friends. Instead, he had nearly wiped out on some back roads and probably stumbled upon a murder victim.

He drew in a deep breath of fresh air to brace himself for what he would find in the trunk. Then he walked around to the rear of the Mercedes.

White lace, stained with blood, spilled over the bumper. He forced himself to look inside the trunk. The woman's face was so pale but for the blood smeared on it. And her long hair, tangled around her head, was nearly as red as her blood.

He recognized the dress, since he had just seen a gown eerily similar to it. But that bride had been alive and happy. This bride was dead. He reached into the trunk to confirm it, his fingers sliding over her throat where her pulse would have been—had she had one any longer.

Something moved beneath his fingertips—in a faint and weak rhythm. He looked down again just as her eyelids fluttered open. Her eyes were a pale, almost silvery, gray, and they were wide with confusion and then fear.

She screamed and struck out, hitting and kicking at him, as she fought him for her life.

THE SCREAM STOPPED him cold, abruptly halting his headlong escape through the forest. He had heard that scream before—seconds before he'd thought he had killed the woman. Hell, he'd been certain he'd killed her.

How could she be alive?

It wasn't possible...

More important, it wasn't acceptable.

He had let the state trooper distract him. With his heart pounding in his chest with fear and nerves, he hadn't known how to react to that police car behind him. At first he'd driven normally, hoping that the trooper wouldn't notice the missing plate—hoping that he would give up following him for some more interesting radio call.

But the trooper must have called in someone else—some other agency—because then he'd noticed the black SUV. And his every instinct had screamed at him to drive as fast as he could—to outrun that vehicle.

Instead, he had let it run him off the road—into that damn ditch. He'd barely escaped the vehicle before the guy had run up to it.

In a tux...

What kind of government agent wore a tuxedo?

The kind that had happened into the wrong situation at the wrong time.

He had to go back. He couldn't leave the woman alive. And if he had to, he would kill the man along with her. And this time, he would make damn certain that she was really dead.

Chapter Two

"It's okay…" The man uttered the claim in a deep voice. "You're safe." But he held a gun in one hand while he grasped her wrists with the other.

His hands were so big that he easily clasped both her wrists in one, restraining her. So she kicked. Or at least she tried. But heavy fabric tangled around her legs, holding her down…inside the trunk of a car.

Fear overwhelmed her as she realized that she had been locked inside that trunk—until this man had opened the lid. She needed to get out; she needed to run. But her head throbbed. A blaring alarm intensified the pain, and her vision blurred as unconsciousness threatened to overwhelm her again. She could barely focus on the man.

He was so big and muscular that he towered over her. Thick dark hair framed a tanned face. And dark eyes stared down at her. He looked as shocked as she felt.

She struggled again, tugging on her wrists

to free them from his grasp. But his hand held her. She fought to move her legs, but they were trapped under the weight of whatever she was wearing.

She glanced down, and all the white nearly blinded her. White lace. White silk. Except for the red spots, which dropped onto the fabric like rain. She was bleeding. Not only had she been locked inside the trunk of a car, she had been wounded.

How badly?

Panic pressed on her, constricting her lungs. But she gathered her strength, opened her mouth and screamed again. Her voice was weak, too, though, and only a soft cry emerged from her throat this time.

"You have no reason to be afraid anymore," the man told her. "You're safe now. You're safe."

Her vision cleared enough that she could see him more clearly. He wore a black jacket with a dark red rose pinned to one of the shiny silk lapels. His shirt was whiter than the dress she was wearing. A black bow tie hung loose around the collar of that shirt.

He was wearing a tuxedo and she was dressed in what had to be a wedding gown. What sick scenario did he have planned for her? Or had it already taken place?

She couldn't remember what had happened and how she had ended up in the trunk of a car.

Since she couldn't change what had already happened, she concentrated instead on the present—on what was happening now and where she was. She peered around him—to the forest surrounding the vehicle that was upended in a ditch. He had brought her to the middle of nowhere.

And she could think of only one reason for that. To dispose of her body…

Because no one would ever find her out here. She had no idea where she was. There were so many trees overhead that she could barely see the sky through the canopy of thick branches. She had no idea which direction was which—even if she was strong enough to escape him. She already knew he was strong from his grip on her wrists; he was so tall and broad shouldered, too.

"Please," she murmured. "Please, don't hurt me…"

She shouldn't have wasted her breath. Uttering those words had cost her so much of what little was left of her strength, and she had no hope of appealing to his sense of humanity. She doubted he had one. He must have been the person who had put her in the trunk, who had hurt her.

He was standing over her, restraining her…and he had the gun. He had to be the one who'd…

But she couldn't remember. She couldn't remember what had happened. The pounding in her head increased as she struggled to summon memories.

But her mind was blank. Completely blank.

She didn't even know who she was....

THE MAN WAS totally focused on the woman—so much so that he would be easily overpowered. And the blaring car alarm would drown out the sound of his approach. Ready to attack, he moved forward, but then sunlight seeped through the thick branches of the trees overhanging the road and glinted off the metal of the weapon the man held.

Just as he'd suspected, this guy wasn't just some Good Samaritan who had happened along to rescue the woman. Despite the tuxedo he was wearing, he had to be some type of lawman. An armed lawman.

Frustration ate at him—joining the bitterness he had always felt for law enforcement. The gun would complicate things. But it wouldn't stop him.

He would enjoy killing the man, too—now that he knew he was in law enforcement. But he would have to act quickly, before any reinforcements arrived.

He had to act now. He had to make sure that the woman really died and the lawman died along with her.

THE PANIC ON the young woman's face struck Dalton like a blow. Those already enormous silvery-gray eyes had widened more with fear while her face had grown even paler.

Aware that he was scaring her, that he was intimidating her, he stepped back. But he was afraid that if he completely released her, she might injure herself as she tried to get away from him. So he continued to hold her wrists.

"Don't move," he cautioned her. As wounded as she was, she shouldn't risk causing more damage to her battered body.

But she ignored his advice and struggled even harder, thrashing about inside the trunk. Maybe she couldn't hear him over the blare of that damn car alarm. But like her, it was growing weaker—probably either as the battery ran down or was damaged from the water flooding the engine, which had already died.

Now he just had to make sure that the bride didn't.

"You're hurt," he told her—in case she hadn't noticed the blood that had stained her dress and made her long hair wet and sticky.

She had lost so much blood that some had even pooled in the trunk beneath her. She needed medical attention as soon as possible. Or he wasn't sure that she would survive.

"You need to hold still," he advised her, "until I get help for you."

But to get help, he would have to put away his gun and take out his cell. He glanced around to see if the driver of the Mercedes had returned. The towering trees cast shadows throughout the woods and onto the gravel road—making the time of day appear closer to night than midafternoon.

The driver could have circled back around—could even now be sneaking up behind them. Dalton peered around—over his shoulder and into the woods, checking for any movement. Sunlight glinted within the trees.

Off a gun?

Or maybe it was a beer can that some teenagers or a hunter had tossed into the woods.

Dalton had spent his life on the streets; he knew what dangers he would face there. He had no idea what lurked out here—where it was so remote. He couldn't see anyone, yet the skin tingled between his shoulder blades. He felt as though he was being watched. Maybe being out of his element was what made him so uneasy—made him reluctant to put away his weapon.

But Dalton had no choice. He had to get help for the battered bride. She had already lost so much blood—maybe too much to survive.

"You're going to be okay." Because he had told

so many over the years, lies came easily to him now. But maybe he wasn't lying; he wasn't a doctor. He had no way of knowing how gravely she was injured, so maybe she would be okay. "But you need to calm down. You need to trust me."

Because of all those lies he'd told and all those old friends from the gang that he had betrayed and arrested, few people trusted him anymore. Certainly no one who knew him.

But he was a stranger to her. Maybe that was why she stopped struggling. Or maybe she was just too weak from all that blood loss.

So he released her wrists, then holstered his weapon and pulled out his cell. But the phone screen blinked out a warning: no signal.

He cursed. He couldn't leave her here while he drove around until his phone had a signal again. She might not survive until he returned. Either her injury might claim her life or the man who'd put her in the trunk might return for her.

Dare Dalton try to move her? To carry her to his SUV and drive her to a hospital? Hell, he didn't even know where a hospital was in this area.

Maybe she wasn't as weak as he'd thought, though, because she drew in an unsteady breath and then tried again to climb out of the trunk. He put a hand on her shoulder to hold her still, though he probably hadn't had to bother. The weight of the blood-soaked dress was already holding down her body.

"You have to take it easy," he warned her. "You have a head injury." At least that looked to be where her blood was coming from. Had she been shot?

In his experience, most of the people he had found in trunks had been shot, execution-style, in the base of the skull. But all of those people had died. If she had a bullet in her head, and he moved her...

She would probably die, too. But if he didn't move her, she still might die. There was too much blood.

She lifted one of her hands and touched her head. Her beautiful face contorted with pain and she jerked her hand back. Staring down at her fingers, which were stained with her own blood, she gasped.

"Do you know what happened?" he asked. Maybe she could tell him if she'd been shot.

But from the dazed and glassy look in her pale gray eyes, she appeared to be in shock. Or maybe it was the injury that had her so groggy and weak.

"Noooo..." she murmured.

Wouldn't she remember being shot? He remembered every time that he had been shot.

"Maybe you were struck over the head," he suggested.

She could have a concussion—some blunt-force trauma that was making her bleed so much. Dalton had seen that kind of injury a lot, too, over the years.

Or she could have been shot from behind, so that she hadn't realized what was happening to her—until it was too late. Until the bullet had been fired into her head.

Gravel scattered across the road, small stones skittering past him and into the water in the gully. Then metal clicked as a gun cocked. And Dalton realized that the same thing had just happened to him. Someone had sneaked up behind him to take him by surprise.

The damn driver must have circled back around—returning to reclaim his victim. To make sure that she was dead and couldn't identify him.

Her eyes widened with shock and fear. Either she could see the man over his shoulder, or she must have heard the gun cocking, too.

Dalton shifted his body slightly, so that he stood between her and the danger. If the man wanted to kill her, he would have to kill Dalton first.

He reached for his holster again—for his gun. But he wouldn't be able to draw it fast enough to save himself from getting shot. But maybe he could get off a shot himself and save her.

Chapter Three

The man had drawn his gun again. But she wasn't afraid *of* him this time. She was afraid *for* him. A shadow had fallen across the road behind him. And that soft click of metal must have been another gun, already cocking…

The bullet would hit the man first—before it hit her. He had positioned himself so that it would. He had positioned himself to protect her.

Maybe he wasn't who or what she'd thought he was. Maybe he wasn't the person who had hurt her. Maybe he wasn't a monster. But how had he found her?

"Who are you?" she whispered. But she wasn't asking for just his name.

"FBI," he identified himself—not to her but to whoever had come up behind him. "Put down your weapon…"

A man uttered a ragged sigh of relief. "Agent Reyes, I couldn't tell if that was you or not…from behind…and in a tux…but of course you were at the wedding…" The man's sigh became a gasp as he peered around the FBI agent and saw her in the trunk. "Is that the bride?"

"No," the agent replied. "Not the bride from the wedding I was at anyway. I don't know who she is. I found her in the car we were pursuing."

Unlike the agent who wore a tuxedo, this man was wearing a vaguely familiar-looking uniform. It was tan and drab like the dust coating the car, but he had a badge pinned to his chest. He was also a law enforcement officer.

She breathed a slight sigh of relief. Maybe she had been rescued—if only she remembered from what…

"Where's the driver?" the state trooper asked. He was shorter and heavier than the agent—with no hair discernible beneath the cap of his hat.

The FBI agent gestured toward the woods. "He ran off before I could even get a look at him. And then I found her in the trunk. She needs medical help."

She heard the urgency in his voice and knew her situation was as critical as she feared it was.

"Does your phone or radio work?" the agent asked the officer. "I can't get a signal."

The other man grabbed at the collar of his shirt and pressed a button on the device attached to it. "We need an ambulance."

They didn't need the ambulance. *She* did. She

had been badly injured. All the blood was hers. No wonder she felt so weak—too weak to even pull herself out of the trunk. Too weak to fight anymore.

"Help's coming," the man called Agent Reyes assured her.

He had already helped her—when he had stopped whoever had been driving the car and opened the trunk for her. She wanted to thank him, but she struggled for the words—for the strength to even move her lips.

"Shh," he said, as if he sensed her struggle. "You're going to get medical attention soon. The ambulance is on its way."

But she was afraid that it would be too late.

"Hang in there," he urged her.

She shook her head and dizziness overwhelmed her, making her stomach pitch and pain reverberate in her head like a chime clanging against the insides of a bell.

"You're strong," he said. Instead of clasping her wrists, he took her hand and squeezed it reassuringly. "You must be strong, or you wouldn't still be alive. You're a fighter. You can hang in there."

She had suspected he was lying to her earlier—when he'd told her she would be okay and especially when he had urged her to trust him. Now she was certain that he was lying. She had never felt weaker than she did right now. At least she didn't think she had...

Memories still eluded her.

"What's your name?" he asked.

She blinked, trying to focus on his face again. He really was quite handsome—with that tanned skin, those dark eyes so heavily lashed and his thick, black hair. It was a little long—longer than she would have thought a government agent would be able to wear his hair.

"What's your name?" he asked again. Moments ago he'd shushed her when she'd tried to talk. Now he was getting insistent, as if he needed her name in case she didn't survive until the ambulance arrived.

She gathered the last of her strength and admitted in a raspy whisper, "I don't know..."

Her memories weren't just eluding her. They were completely gone, as if they had seeped out with her blood—leaving her mind entirely blank.

"I don't know..." she murmured again...just as oblivion returned to claim her.

"WHERE'S THAT DAMN AMBULANCE?" Dalton demanded to know. Maybe the trooper had called only minutes ago for help, but it felt like hours—with the young woman lying unconscious in the trunk of the car.

Dalton had pressed her veil onto the wound on

the back of her head, trying to stem the bleeding. But the fabric was flimsy.

Trooper Littlefield pointed down the gravel road where he must have abandoned his squad car, since he'd come up behind Reyes on foot. "I can hear them coming now."

The faint whine of sirens reached his ears, too. And in the distance a cloud of dust rose up into the trees.

"Help's coming," he told the woman, hoping that she could hear him even though she was unconscious. "Stay with me. Help's coming."

Then he turned back toward Littlefield. The trooper was older than him—shorter and heavier. And he was sweating so badly that it streaked from his bald head down his neck to stain the collar of his tan shirt. He probably hadn't chosen to walk the rest of the way down the gravel road. Had he crashed? Or had the car just overheated from the chase?

"Can they get around your car?" he asked.

He nodded. "I parked it off to the side—" he gestured toward the FBI SUV "—like you did."

Dalton hadn't exactly parked there; he had just been fortunate enough to have ended up there instead of in the ditch like the Mercedes had.

"Why did you abandon your car?" Dalton asked.

The trooper pointed toward the Mercedes. "I

heard the cars stop. I wasn't sure what the situation was…" He glanced at the woman in the trunk. "I didn't think it would be this, though."

Despite all those bodies Dalton had found in car trunks over the years, this wasn't the situation he had expected, either. It was just too ironic and coincidental since he'd just been at a wedding himself that he would find a bride locked inside a trunk. Then he remembered that conversation he'd had outside the church—the one with profiler Special Agent Jared Bell.

Could this bride have been the next intended victim of Bell's serial killer?

As far as he knew, the guy hadn't killed another woman for a couple of years. He wouldn't claim this victim, either—if Dalton could do anything about it.

Finally the sirens grew louder and lights flashed as the ambulance approached. "Help's here," he told her. "You're going to be okay."

Her lashes fluttered, and she peered at him through her barely opened lids. "Don't lie to me."

"Help really is here." And as he said it, paramedics rushed up to the car. He released the blood-soaked veil to one of them and then he tried to release her hand—that he hadn't even realized he still held—and step back out of their way.

But she clasped his hand tightly in hers. She was stronger than she thought—stronger even than he had thought. "Don't leave me," she implored him.

Recently another agent had nearly lost a witness at the hospital when bank robbery suspects had tried to abduct her right out of the ER. Dalton wasn't about to take that risk. This woman had already been through too much.

"I need to ride along," he told the paramedics. Then he told her, "I won't leave you."

Her eyes closed again. Somehow she trusted him—when she had no reason to trust him or anyone else after what had happened to her. What exactly had happened to her?

"Was she shot?" he asked the paramedic who eased the veil away from her head wound.

The young man shrugged. "I don't know. They'll get a CT scan in the ER. So we need to get her to the hospital ASAP." He and another man snapped a collar around her neck and then lifted her onto a board that they carried up to the gurney they'd left on the road.

Dalton had to run along beside the stretcher they rolled along the gravel road to the ambulance. He hurried inside the rig just as they closed the doors and sped away. From their urgency, it was clear that her condition was every bit as critical as Dalton had feared it was.

"How far from the hospital are we?" he asked.

"Twenty minutes out," the driver replied.

He would bet every one of those minutes counted in her situation. The paramedic in the back had administered an IV and an oxygen mask. It was more than he had been able to offer her. But it wasn't enough. Not if there was a bullet in her head.

"What is her name?" the paramedic asked.

"She doesn't know," Dalton replied. "Could she have amnesia?"

"It's possible if she has a concussion," the paramedic replied. "But what is her name?"

"She couldn't tell me," he pointed out, "so I don't know."

"You're not her groom?"

A strange shiver rushed over him. "Of course not. I'm an FBI agent. I found her in the trunk of that car."

The paramedic glanced down at Dalton's tux and nodded, as if humoring him.

"I just came from a wedding," he explained his attire. "It wasn't mine."

It would never be his.

"I don't know who she is," he repeated. But maybe something had been left in the trunk of the car that would have revealed her identity. A purse. A wallet. A receipt. Or the registration for the car that might have been hers.

He should have stayed behind at the scene. He could have done more for her there than by playing nursemaid in the back of the ambulance. And why would the man who'd put her in that trunk risk showing up at the hospital?

If the guy was smart, he was still running.

"What the hell…" the driver murmured from the front seat.

Dalton glanced up and peered out the windshield—at the police car barreling down the road toward them with lights flashing and sirens blaring.

"Does he want me to pull over?" the driver asked as he reached for the radio on the dash. "Why doesn't he tell me what he wants?"

Another shiver rushed over Dalton, this one so deep that it chilled his blood. They hadn't passed the trooper's abandoned vehicle. He had a bad feeling that it was that vehicle heading straight toward them now.

But it was not Trooper Littlefield driving it. It wasn't the bald man behind the vehicle. This person had a hat pulled low over his face. But that wasn't the reason he was driving straight toward them. He wanted to run them off the road; he wanted to reclaim the victim who had nearly escaped him.

The ambulance driver jerked the wheel and veered toward one of those deep ditches. At the last moment, he jerked the wheel back and kept the rig on the road, riding along the steep shoulder. "What the hell's that trooper doing?"

"It's not the trooper." It had to be the man who'd run from the Mercedes. He must have circled back around and found the trooper's abandoned vehicle. "And don't pull over…"

"But he's going to kill us!" the other paramedic exclaimed. "He's heading straight toward us!"

But the man couldn't have expected that an FBI agent was riding along in the rig. So Dalton had the element of surprise. He pulled his gun from his holster, leaned forward over the passenger's seat and pointed the barrel out the open passenger's window.

Maybe the man saw the gun, because he sped up as if trying to run them off the road before Dalton could fire a shot. Dust billowed up behind the trooper's car, forming a cloud thicker than fog. Dalton could barely see through it, but he fired his weapon. Again and again.

He couldn't tell if he struck the car, though—let alone the driver. And the vehicle kept coming toward them. Faster and faster.

The ambulance driver cursed.

"Keep going straight," Dalton advised him. The road was too narrow; the ditches too deep and the gravel too loose. "Don't swerve."

But his warning came too late.

The ambulance driver didn't have the nerves for

the dangerous game of chicken. Cursing, he jerked the wheel, and the rig teetered on two wheels.

The paramedic in the back shouted in fear.

The driver couldn't regain control of the van and it flipped—over and over—hurtling Dalton over the seat and toward the windshield. If he went through it—if he lost consciousness—he risked losing the bride…

But then the accident would probably be enough to finish her off. She was already critically wounded. He held his breath and tried to brace himself.

But it was too late.

THE AMBULANCE LAY crumpled on its side in the ditch, but its lights flashed and sirens blared yet. With a gloved hand, he turned off the lights and sirens inside the state police cruiser. But he could hear an echo of the ambulance's sirens in the distance.

More emergency vehicles were on their way to the scene. Maybe the trooper had called for more help. Maybe the agent had managed to get a call out before the ambulance had crashed. The agent was inside that crashed vehicle. He'd seen him climb into the ambulance with the woman—determined to protect her.

The agent had even shot at him; the windshield of the police cruiser bore holes too close to where his head had been. He shuddered at how close those shots had come to hitting him. Even with both vehicles moving, the agent had nearly struck him. He was a damn good shot. A dangerous man.

Maybe that was why he hesitated before approaching that crumpled ambulance. He didn't know what he would find inside: dead bodies or a still-armed government agent.

The ambulance sirens grew weaker, while those sirens in the distance grew louder as those vehicles approached. He could hesitate no longer. He had to hurry. Before the other emergency personnel arrived, he had to make certain that both the woman and the lawman were dead.

HER HEART AND her head pounded with fear and pain. Strapped to the gurney, she had actually taken little impact from the crash. Since the gurney was anchored to the floor, she hadn't been thrown around like the others.

The blond-haired paramedic who'd been in the back with her had bounced around like a rag doll and then crumpled against the side of the ambulance where it had come to rest in the deep ditch next to the road.

She couldn't tell if the man was just unconscious.

Or…

A cry burned her throat, but she held it in—refusing to panic. Yet.

Strapped down and hanging on her side, she could only twist her neck to peer around the vehicle—to see what had happened to the others. To the FBI agent.

The driver was pinned beneath the steering wheel, so he remained in his seat. Like the other paramedic, he wasn't moving. How badly was he hurt?

They had come to help her. But now they needed help. Because of her?

Guilt struck her with all the force that the ambulance had struck the ditch. Could this be her fault?

Could she have done something to cause this destruction—this pain? How much destruction?

She craned her neck, but she couldn't see the agent. Had he catapulted out of the windshield? The glass was broken. But then, he might have shot it out. He had been shooting—trying to stop the other vehicle from running them off the road. According to the paramedics' comments, the other vehicle had been a police car.

The trooper's uniform had looked vaguely familiar to her. Had she seen him before? Was he the one who'd put her in the trunk?

Was there anyone she could trust? Special Agent Reyes had done his best to save her. But where was he now? Pinned beneath the vehicle when it had rolled?

She shuddered as she imagined the worst. And her head throbbed more with dull pain. The pounding wasn't just inside her head, though.

Someone was hammering on the back doors of the ambulance—trying to open them. She struggled against the straps, but they held her fast to the gurney. She couldn't move—she couldn't escape. She could only wait for whoever had run them off the road to finish her off.

Chapter Four

Water seeped through the tuxedo, chilling Dalton's skin. He awoke with a jerk—then grunted as his head slammed against metal. Stars danced behind his eyes as oblivion threatened to reclaim him. But then he heard the hammering and felt the force of it rocking the ambulance.

Fortunately he wasn't beneath the vehicle. Instead of going through the windshield, he had grabbed hold of the dash and had somehow wound up wedged beneath it—between the passenger's seat and the door. Water surged through that door from where the van lay on its side in the ditch. If he hadn't awakened, he may have drowned.

But now, as the doors creaked and finally gave, he still could die because he had no intention of letting anyone hurt the injured woman more than she had already been hurt. He fumbled around on the wet floor, looking for his gun. Finally his fingers grazed metal. He closed his hand around it, but the barrel was stuck—wedged between the seat and the crumpled passenger door.

As he tugged on the Glock, he lifted his head to assess the situation. The bride, strapped to the gurney, was suspended on her side. Her silvery-gray eyes were open and wide with fear. She knew she was trapped. Then she noticed him.

And he saw hope brighten her face, infusing her pallid skin with a hint of color. Of life…

She was okay now.

But he wasn't sure how much hope he offered her—when he couldn't get his damn gun loose. So he turned away from her to focus on those opening doors. And he released his breath in a ragged sigh of relief.

WHEN THOSE AMBULANCE doors jerked open, Dalton had been relieved to see—along with his friends Blaine and Ash—Jared Bell. Now he was worried rather than relieved. While the FBI profiler hadn't said much of anything in the hour since he had arrived at the accident scene, Dalton was pretty sure the man was going to try to snag his case and his witness.

As Dalton rushed into the hospital emergency room, he realized he was more concerned about losing the witness than the case. That concern worried him more. She was easy to find in the small rural hospital; two troopers stood outside the curtain where she was, while the blond FBI agent stood guard next to her bed.

"Is she okay?" he asked Blaine.

Dalton had managed to talk Ash into returning to his wedding, but that hadn't eased much of his guilt over disrupting the reception. Unfortunately, the other agents had heard the trooper's call for an ambulance and thought Dalton was the one needing medical attention. That was why they had all showed up when they had—at the perfect moment.

But none of them had caught the man who had driven the ambulance off the road. He had escaped them just as easily as he had escaped Dalton. And just like Dalton, no one had even gotten a glimpse of him.

In response to Dalton's question, Blaine shook his head. Dread had Dalton's stomach plummeting.

"Is she…?" He turned toward the bed where she was lying, her wedding gown replaced with a hospital gown. The blood washed away from her face, it was devoid of all color now. But her red hair was vibrant against the pillow and sheets. She couldn't be gone.

Wouldn't they have covered her face, her beautiful face, if she were dead?

"God, no, she's not," Blaine hastened to assure

him. "But the doctors are concerned about her head injury."

"Why isn't she in surgery, then?" he asked.

He shouldn't have stayed behind at the accident scene with Agent Bell. He should have ridden in the second ambulance, which had arrived to replace the crashed one, with the victim and the injured paramedics. But because he had stayed behind, he had been able to point out things to Bell that the man might not have noticed on his own—like how both the Mercedes and the trooper's car had been hot-wired.

Had Bell's serial killer known how to do that?

But then, Dalton's car thieves had never taken a hostage before.

Whose case was this?

Her heavy lashes fluttered against her cheeks as she lifted her lids and stared at him. "You're back…" Her breath shuddered out with relief.

Relief eased the tightness in his chest. She wasn't dead…

"Where are these doctors?" he asked Blaine. But he didn't look around for the ER physicians; he couldn't pull his gaze from hers.

"She doesn't need surgery," Blaine said.

"But the head wound…" If her head was bandaged, it must have been beneath her hair, because he couldn't see any gauze or tape. "It isn't a GSW?"

Blaine replied, "She wasn't shot."

Dalton uttered a sigh of relief—which Bell echoed. Until now, the profiler had barely paid any attention to the victim. Of course, as a profiler, he was all about the perp. Did he intend to link this case—and her—to his serial killer?

"I have a concussion," she said. "The neuro specialist said that's probably why I can't remember…"

"You can't remember?" Bell asked. "Anything…?"

She glanced at him but turned back to Dalton, as if seeking assurance that she could trust the stranger. Earlier he had convinced her that she could trust Blaine. Hell, Blaine Campbell was well-known for his protectiveness. Dalton wouldn't have trusted her safety to anyone else—not with a man out there determined to kill her.

Dalton hesitated only a moment before nodding that she could trust Bell, too. The guy was legendary for his intelligence and determination. Only one killer had escaped him in all the years he'd been a profiler.

"I don't remember anything," she said. "But him…" She lifted her hand toward Dalton. "I just remember him lifting the trunk lid…"

"Nothing else?" Bell asked. "You don't remember anything that happened before that?"

She closed her eyes as if searching her mind for memories. Or maybe she was just exhausted.

"She's in no condition for an interrogation right now," he admonished Bell.

"The doctors said her concussion is serious," Blaine added. "She lost a lot of blood from the head wound, too, so she's really physically weak."

Her eyes opened again. "I am not weak."

"She's not," Dalton agreed. Just as he had told her earlier, he repeated, "She's very strong." She had survived two attempts on her life.

"I could handle an interrogation," she said. "I would love to answer your questions—all of your questions—if I had any answers. But I can't tell you anything about how I wound up in that trunk. I can't even tell you my name."

Tears glistened in her eyes, but she blinked furiously, fighting them back. He suspected they were tears of frustration. He couldn't imagine losing all of his memories—to the extent that he didn't even know his name. As he had when she'd been bleeding in the trunk, he reached out and clasped her hand. At that time he had been urging her to hold on to life; now he wanted her to hold on to him.

She clutched at his hand and squeezed. "Since you can't interrogate me, I'm going to interrogate all of you. I need answers. I need to know who I am and what happened to me."

He had been right about her. She was strong—hopefully strong enough to handle the truth, whatever it was.

"Does she have any other injuries?" he asked Blaine.

"I remember what the doctor told me," she informed him. "I just don't remember anything before you opened that trunk."

He didn't want to upset her by asking her how else she might have been injured, but it was important to know what kind of attacker they were dealing with. A sexual predator? Anger coursed through him. He wanted to find this guy. And he wanted to hurt him for hurting *her*.

"What are your other injuries?" Jared Bell asked the question now, no doubt because he was trying to profile her attacker.

She shivered even though a few blankets covered her hospital gown. He squeezed her hand, offering comfort and reassurance, and she offered him a smile. God, she was beautiful—so beautiful that his breath stuck in his lungs for a moment.

"What you're thinking," she said, "it didn't happen." She shuddered now—in revulsion at the thought and in relief. "I have some bumps, bruises and scrapes—"

"In addition to the head injury and amnesia," Blaine finished for her.

"Amnesia," she bitterly repeated. "I need to know who I am. You're all in the FBI. You must know *something* about me."

"Contrary to public opinion," Blaine said, "we don't have files on everyone. So we don't know your identity. We don't know anything yet."

"We checked the missing person's report in the area," Agent Bell said. "No one's reported a bride missing."

She glanced at Blaine and then Jared Bell before focusing on him again. "None of you have any answers," she said with a ragged sigh of resignation and weariness. "You don't know who I am or why I was in the trunk of that car, either."

"We don't," Dalton admitted.

"So what do I call myself?" she asked. And now her voice sounded weak, thready, as exhaustion threatened to claim her.

"Jane Doe," Blaine suggested.

She wrinkled her nose in distaste. "That makes it sound like I didn't survive. Like I'm a dead body."

Dalton had another suggestion. But he didn't want to upset her. "We'll find out your real name," he said. "And how you wound up in that trunk. I promise you that we will find out." He squeezed her hand again.

While she wasn't weak, she was exhausted, and her eyes closed again as sleep claimed her.

"You shouldn't have made her any promises," Jared Bell admonished him.

"Why not?" Because the profiler intended to steal the case from him?

"It isn't like you," Blaine agreed. "You always swear you're not going to make *anyone* any promises. You're never getting married."

"I'm not marrying anyone," Dalton anxiously corrected him. That was a promise he'd made himself long ago. "I'm just going to find out who she is and how she wound up in that trunk."

"But if nobody reports her missing and she doesn't have DNA on file, there might not be any way to find out who she is," Bell cautioned him. "You can't risk putting her picture out there. You can't risk a news report about her."

"I wouldn't risk it," Dalton assured him. He couldn't risk kooks coming out of the woodwork trying to claim they knew her or cared about her—not in her vulnerable state.

"Why not?" Blaine asked. "Her attacker obviously knows she's still alive, or he wouldn't have tried running the ambulance off the road."

Jared Bell shook his head. "The last thing her attacker needs is any publicity…"

Dalton wasn't worried about her attacker; he was worried about her.

"But it might be the only way," Blaine said,

"since the doctors said she might never regain her memory."

Even while his heart sank for her, Dalton shrugged. "It doesn't matter. *I* will still find out who she is and what happened to her." And he would find out without putting her in even more danger.

SHE MIGHT NEVER regain her memory.

She had only closed her eyes to hold back more tears—not to sleep. So she'd heard what the agent had said.

She had already heard the doctor say it, too, though, so the pronouncement wasn't a shock. But hearing it again made it more real. She might never remember her life before the moment that Special Agent Dalton Reyes had opened the car trunk and rescued her.

Her oldest memory was of him—standing over her looking all handsome in his black tuxedo with his bow tie lying loose around his neck. If not for the trunk and the concussion and the blood, it might not have been such a bad memory. He was such an attractive man. But he wasn't just a man. To her, he had become a hero.

The FBI agents must not have realized that she wasn't sleeping, because they spoke freely over her—as if she wasn't there. Since she didn't remember who she was, it was almost as if she didn't really exist.

She had no name. No history.

"You didn't find anything at the crime scene to reveal her identity?" It must have been the blond man—Agent Campbell—who'd asked, since he had been the one assigned to protect her in the second ambulance. Fortunately, the paramedics from the first ambulance had had only minor injuries from the crash. They'd ridden along with her, too, to the hospital.

"No," Dalton replied. "The glove box was empty, and there was no license plate on the car. I'll have to run the vehicle identification number to find out whose name it was titled in last."

Hers?

She hadn't even seen the vehicle. She had no idea in what kind of trunk she had been found.

"The car was hot-wired, though—like Trooper Littlefield's patrol car had been," he continued. "This guy's a pro."

"So you think he's part of that ring of car thieves you've been tracking?" Agent Campbell asked.

"Definitely."

"Have your car thieves taken a hostage before?" the other man asked. Back at the crash site Dalton had introduced him as Agent Bell.

She could remember all of their names; it was her own she couldn't recall.

Dalton said nothing in reply to Agent Bell's question before the man asked another. "And would they risk returning to the scene to reclaim that hostage?"

Now Dalton cursed. "I know what you're up to," he said, as if he was accusing the other agent of something nefarious. "You're going to try to make this your case."

She almost opened her eyes then so that she could protest. She wanted Special Agent Reyes on her case—and not just because he'd promised to find out who she was and what had happened.

Maybe it was because her oldest memory was of him—maybe it was because he had saved her life—that she felt so connected to him. Even dependent on him...

She had no sense of herself. Her only sense was of him. But the only thing she actually knew about him was that he was an FBI special agent. She knew nothing of his life. She'd heard him say he was never getting married, but that didn't mean he wasn't involved with someone. That he didn't have kids.

"I hope it's not my case, Reyes," the other man replied with grave brevity. "I don't want to think that he's back—that he's killing again..."

"She's not dead," Dalton said.

"She would have been—if you hadn't stopped him," Agent Bell said. "But you didn't really stop him. He came back and hot-wired the trooper's car. He tried again."

"But he didn't kill her," Dalton said. "It's not him—it's not your serial killer. Or she would be dead. Some of his victims may not have been found, but nobody's ever escaped him. It's not the Bride Butcher."

Bride Butcher...

The words chilled her, but she suppressed a shiver and a shudder of horror and recognition. The name sounded vaguely but frighteningly familiar to her.

But why would the killer be after her? She was no bride. Then she realized there was a slight weight on her left hand, something hard and metallic encircling her ring finger. Was she engaged? Married?

"I hope it's not him," Agent Bell said again, "because if it is, he'll keep trying until he kills her."

So she might not have lost only her memory. She could still lose her life...

BY THE TIME he had made it to the hospital where she'd been taken, the place was crawling with FBI agents and state troopers—just as the crash site had been.

He had just about had those crumpled doors of the ambulance open when those other vehicles had arrived on the scene. He'd slipped back into the woods just as two men dressed in tuxedos, like the dark-haired agent, and another dressed in a suit had rushed to the aid and protection of the crash victims.

He had moved too quickly into the concealment of the dense forest for them to see him. And they had been too preoccupied with rescuing the others to notice him watching them.

The way he was watching them now—at the small hospital near the Lake Michigan shoreline. There were so many of them: agents and state troopers and even some county deputies for added security. So he would have to be careful—because he was damn well not going to get caught.

So he would have to bide his time until the perfect opportunity presented itself. And, eventually, it would. He wasn't going to give up; he wouldn't stop until he had finished this.

Until he had finished *her*…

But now *she* wasn't the only one he wanted dead. He had to kill the FBI special agent, too. He would probably even need to kill him first—since the man had assigned himself the woman's hero.

In order for him to get to her again, the agent would probably have to be eliminated first. But the order didn't particularly matter to him. All that mattered was that he had to make certain that both the woman and her hero died.

Chapter Five

He watched her from the doorway. She was awake now. But she didn't see him. Instead, she was staring down at her hand, studying the diamond on it. Either she was admiring the big square stone or she was trying to remember where the hell it had come from.

Her memory was really gone. He had spoken with the doctors, too, and had confirmed everything that Blaine Campbell had told him yesterday. Now if only Dalton could confirm what Jared Bell had told him.

If she really had been abducted by the Bride Butcher serial killer, then Dalton should turn the case over to the profiler. Jared Bell knew the case best.

But Jared Bell hadn't caught the killer when he'd had the chance before. And he had made no promises that he would catch him now.

Dalton was the one who had made her the promises. Dalton and probably whoever had put that ring on her finger. She had been wearing a bridal gown. Was she married? Or was she only engaged? Who was the man in her life and why hadn't he filed a missing persons report for her?

Dalton had checked, but he had found no report for anyone matching her description. Midtwenties, five foot seven or eight inches tall, red haired, breathtakingly beautiful...

If he was the man who had put the ring on her finger, he wouldn't have just reported her missing; he would have been out looking for her—desperate to find her.

But maybe the man who had put the ring on her finger had also put her in the trunk. Dalton had a name now—for the owner of the vehicle. He also had an address. But to follow up the lead, he would have to leave her to someone else's protection.

Blaine's? Or Agent Bell's? Or Trooper Littlefield's? The guy hadn't left his keys in his patrol car; he hadn't done anything wrong. He deserved a chance to prove himself, but not at any risk to her...

"Do you have bad news for me?" she asked. "Is that why you're reluctant to come into my room?"

A grin tugged at his lips. The woman kept surprising him—with her strength and with her intuitiveness. He hadn't thought she'd even noticed him watching her. However, she apparently didn't miss much. But her memories.

He stepped inside the hospital room and walked closer to her bed. She was sitting up, and thanks to the IV in her arm, she had more color. She looked healthier. Stronger…

"I have no news for you," he said.

She sighed. "Well, that is bad, then."

"How about you?" he asked. "Any memories?"

Had staring at that diamond brought anything rushing back to her? Any feeling of love for whoever had given her the engagement ring?

She shook her head and then flinched at the motion.

Concern gripped him. "Still in pain?"

"Not so much thanks to the painkillers they've been giving me," she said. "It's just a dull ache now unless I make any sharp movements."

"You are tough," he mused.

The doctor had said that someone had given her quite a blow—probably with a pipe or a golf club. It had lacerated her skin and fractured her skull. But the fracture had probably actually saved her life since it had relieved the pressure and released the blood of what could have been a dangerous subdural hematoma. That was why there had been so much blood. But transfusions had replaced what she'd lost. According to the doctor, she was doing extremely well.

"I am tough," she said. "So you can tell me about this *no* news. What do you mean?"

Hopefully, she was tough enough to deal with the facts, because he wasn't going to keep anything from her. There was already too much that she didn't know—that she couldn't remember.

So he replied, "Nobody has filed a missing persons report for anyone matching your description."

She flinched again, but she hadn't even moved her head. This pain was emotional. "So no one is missing me."

"I doubt that's the case," he said—because he would have missed her, had he not known where she was, and he barely knew her. "I'm sure there's another explanation."

"Like what?" she challenged him.

And because he believed she was strong, he told her the truth. "Your groom could have been the one who put you in the trunk of that car."

"You think I'm married?" she asked as she glanced down at that ring again.

"I don't know." But part of him hoped she wasn't—the part that had his heart racing over how beautiful she was. Her red hair was so vibrant and her silvery-gray eyes so sharp with intelligence and strength.

"Because this looks like just a solitaire engagement ring," she said. "There's no wedding band soldered to it. So I don't think I'm married."

"She's right," a female voice agreed.

Even if Dalton hadn't recognized the voice, he wouldn't have been too worried about someone slipping past Security and getting to her room. He had a guard stationed near the elevators, so no one would get onto the floor without getting checked out.

The only one who was in danger from this woman was him—for disrupting her wedding the day before. He braced himself, for her understandable and justified anger, before turning toward the doorway.

Their arms wound around each other, the bride stood next to her groom. But unlike Dalton, they had changed out of their wedding clothes. Claire wore a bright blue sundress, while Ash wore jeans and a T-shirt. Of course, more than a day had passed since the ceremony.

Dalton really needed to return the damn tuxedo. And shower…

"Aren't you two supposed to be on your honeymoon?" he asked. He hoped he hadn't disrupted that, too.

"We're on our way to the airport," Ash assured him. From how tightly he held her, he looked as if he couldn't wait to get his bride alone again. "But Claire wanted to stop by and check on you."

"I'm fine," he said.

She clicked her tongue against her teeth, admonishing his dismissiveness. "You were in an accident."

"It was no accident." The man driving the trooper's vehicle had intended to run them off the road.

"That's even worse," she said.

"I'm fine," he said again.

Color rushed to the blonde's pale-skinned face. "Good. Now I feel a little less guilty for threatening your life when I realized you ditched our wedding to chase down a stolen car."

He didn't blame her for being angry with him and could just imagine the words she had probably silently mouthed about him. "I'm sorry, Claire."

She pulled away from her husband, rushed forward and hugged Dalton. "I'm so glad that you did." Then she turned toward the bed and smiled at the patient.

"I'm glad, too," the red-haired woman said, "since he saved my life."

"He does that," Claire said. "Saving lives is kind of his thing." She moved closer to the bed and extended her hand. "I'm Claire Stryker."

Ash chuckled. "She keeps introducing herself to everyone—even her dad."

The redhead took Claire's hand in hers. "I wish I could tell you my name, but…"

"You really don't remember anything?" Claire asked.

"No."

"We will find out who you are." Dalton reiterated the promise that, according to Jared Bell, he'd had no business making. "But in the meantime, we need to call you something." Besides *redhead*…

"Special Agent Campbell suggested Jane Doe," she reminded him. "I guess that is what unidentified females are called…" But she hadn't liked it because Jane Doe usually referred to unidentified dead bodies.

But he'd thought she was dead when he had first opened that trunk. He resisted the urge to shudder at the thought of her being dead.

"We could call you Mercedes," he suggested. He had hesitated to bring it up the day before, but it was better than Jane Doe.

"Mercedes?" she and Claire asked in unison.

"It's the kind of car he found her in," Ash explained. "Of course Reyes would go with the name of a car."

He whistled in appreciation of the vintage Mercedes. "She was a beautiful car…" Before she'd been put in the ditch. And now he knew who owned her. The car. He hoped that there was no guy out there who thought he owned the woman. But she had been put in the trunk like so much baggage...

Claire's blond brows drew together as she considered the choices. "Jane or Mercedes?"

The redhead shrugged as if she didn't care what they called her. "It doesn't matter."

"We need to find out your real name," Claire said.

"We will," Dalton said, but he felt a frisson of unease over how easily he was tossing out these promises. He had never been *that* guy—like Blaine or Ash. He wasn't the marine. He wasn't the hero. He was just the guy who worked hard because his job was his life. It was all he had. It was all he wanted, though.

"I'm really good with computers," Claire said, which was a gross understatement of her world-renowned hacking skills. "Maybe I could do some digging—"

"I already have a team on it," Dalton said. "They're using facial recognition to try to link her to online media pictures. It's being handled, and you two have a plane to catch."

"You sure you don't want our help?" Ash asked. His offer sounded sincere, but Dalton wouldn't blame him if it wasn't.

Selfishly, he would love their help. Claire was a genius and Ash was a legendary agent and former marine. But there was no way that Dalton would mess up any more of the Strykers' plans. They had been through hell to earn their much-deserved happiness.

"I doubt this has anything to do with terrorism or national security," Dalton said—since that was Ash Stryker's specialty with the Bureau.

"Then maybe Jared Bell is who you need," Ash suggested.

The redhead shook her head again despite the fact that the motion had her wincing in pain. Then she turned toward Claire. "You agreed with me," she said. "You agreed that I'm not married. So if I'm not a bride, I couldn't be a victim of the Bride Butcher."

She had heard them yesterday. He'd thought she was sleeping, but she had heard everything he and Blaine and Jared Bell had said in her room. Now he flinched—with regret. He didn't want to keep anything from her, but there were some things she hadn't had to hear...like anything about the sadistic serial killer.

If that was who had abducted her, it was probably better that she never remembered what had happened to her. She would never recover from the nightmare of confronting such a monster.

PANIC OVERWHELMED HER, stealing away her breath. But she was actually less afraid of having a serial killer after her than she was afraid of losing Agent Reyes. He couldn't pass off her case to someone else.

"The victims of the Bride Butcher aren't married yet," Agent Stryker said. "He abducts the women at their last fitting for their wedding dress."

She shook her head—not in denial of what he claimed but in denial that she could have been at a fitting for a wedding dress. "No..."

"Do you remember something?" Claire Stryker asked. "Something that makes you think you're not really engaged?"

"I can't remember anything..." She stared at the newly married couple. Their love was palpable—like another presence in the hospital room. "But if I was married or engaged, wouldn't I remember...*him*?"

"Maybe you don't want to remember," Dalton suggested. He apparently suspected that was who had hurt her.

Was she such a horrible judge of character that she would have fallen in love with a monster?

The petite blonde stepped closer to the bed and reached for her hand. She twisted the ring on her finger.

"What are you thinking?" she asked. Such intelligence shone in Claire's eyes that she wanted to hear her opinion.

"It looks like this ring has been on your finger for a while," the other woman replied.

Her stomach pitched. And yet the person who'd put that ring on her hand hadn't even filed a missing persons report for her? What kind of man was her fiancé? The monster Dalton Reyes apparently suspected he was?

Agent Stryker glanced at his watch and said, "If we're going to make our flight, we should get going…"

"We should stay," Claire told her husband. "We could help…"

"You could," Dalton agreed. "But you're not. You're going to leave for your honeymoon and have a wonderful time."

Claire hesitated.

Even her husband looked uncertain. "Let's talk in the hall a moment…"

Her stomach sank again as the two men stepped out of the room. She was certain that Agent Stryker was going to try to talk Dalton into handing her case over to Agent Bell.

"Don't worry," Claire told her. "We only offered to help because we owe him—not because we don't think he's capable of solving the case on his own. Dalton is a very good agent."

She nodded in agreement. "I know. I wouldn't be alive if he wasn't."

"He's not like Ash and Blaine Campbell,

though," Claire continued. "They were marines—they grew up knowing what was right and what was wrong."

Anger surged through her, and she opened her mouth to defend him. The special agent obviously knew what was right and wrong.

But before she could speak, Claire continued, "Dalton grew up on the streets—in a gang. He had to figure out for himself what was right and wrong. I think that's even more impressive."

"So do I," she said. But everything about Dalton Reyes impressed her. She couldn't help wondering about herself. What kind of person was she? Was she an honorable person? Did she know right from wrong?

"This must be so hard for you," Claire said, "not having your memories. Not knowing how you grew up—who your family is or your friends…"

She wondered if she had any—since nobody had filed a report about her missing. Dalton and Agent Stryker stepped back into the room, and like the love between the Strykers, there was love between the men—a strong bond of friendship.

Her heart ached with an overwhelming sense of loss. But she hadn't just lost her friends; she had lost herself, as well.

Dalton uttered a long-suffering sigh, even while his dark eyes twinkled with merriment. "I had to give this guy some advice for the honeymoon." He turned toward Claire. "You're welcome."

The new bride laughed. "Like *you* have any experience with honeymoons or will *ever* have any experience…"

Apparently, as well as growing up on the streets, Dalton had grown up determined to remain single. She hadn't been surprised when she'd overheard him telling Blaine Campbell that he wasn't marrying anyone. Ever. She faintly remembered him saying something in the ambulance when the paramedic had mistaken her for his bride. She'd been in and out of consciousness, so she hadn't picked up on his words but on his tone. He had been appalled that someone had mistaken him for a groom.

At the moment she could relate as she glanced down at her hand again. She wanted to take off the ring. She couldn't believe she was engaged. It didn't feel right.

"If you two don't get going, you won't have any honeymoon experience, either," Dalton warned them.

Claire glanced at her. "But I could help…"

"I have help," Dalton said. He wrapped his arm around the young bride and steered her toward the doorway. "I know you two can't stand spending time together, but you're going to have to suck it up for the next fifty or sixty years."

The newlyweds chuckled—confident in their love and their relationship.

She glanced down at her ring again. Why would she be wearing this when she obviously hadn't felt that way about whoever had put the ring on her finger? But then, a love like the Strykers' was rare and special.

"It was nice meeting you," Claire called back to her.

She had met Claire. She wasn't sure if they'd met her—because she wasn't sure who she was, except not Jane or Mercedes. But maybe she would need to start thinking of herself as one of those names since she was unlikely to ever remember her own. She waved at them. "Enjoy your honeymoon."

The Strykers both hugged Dalton before leaving. He stared after them a moment, as if tempted to call them back, before he turned back to her.

"Who is your help?" she asked. While it would have been selfish to keep them from their honeymoon, she would have trusted the Strykers to help her.

"Trooper Littlefield is going to stand guard in your room," he told her, "while I go to Chicago to follow up a lead."

"Littlefield?" she asked.

Was that the trooper whose car had been stolen? Because of that and because something about him or his uniform was vaguely, unsettlingly familiar to her, she wouldn't feel particularly safe with him. But then, she didn't feel particularly safe with anyone but Dalton.

"He's a good officer," Dalton assured her. "He's the one who called me when he noticed the vintage Mercedes. He knew something wasn't right about it."

Her in the trunk—that was what hadn't been right about it. What if he hadn't seen the car? What if Dalton hadn't stopped it?

She would be dead. She was certain of it. She shuddered with the realization that someone out there wanted her dead. What kind of person was she that someone could hate her enough to try to kill her more than once…?

"Are you okay?" Dalton asked, his voice even deeper with concern. "Claire didn't upset you, did she?"

She shook her head. Claire hadn't upset her, but meeting the other woman had. "I just wish…"

"What?" he asked.

"I wish I knew what kind of person I am," she said. "If I'm like her…" Or if she was someone who'd earned another person's hatred? "I just wish I knew who I am…"

"You may not know your name," Dalton said, "but you know who are you are—you're strong and smart and brave."

But she felt like none of those things. She was terrified—terrified of the person determined to kill her, terrified to be away from Dalton Reyes and terrified to find out who she really was.

ALL HE'D HAD to do was bide his time. Eventually the dark-haired agent had left—along with the other federal agents. They weren't bodyguards; they were investigators.

He wasn't worried about what they would find. He'd been careful so that nothing could be traced back to him. Not even her...

But still she had to die.

And it would be easier for him to kill her now that the agent was gone. He'd left behind the bald-headed trooper for her protection.

All he'd had to do was wait him out. With the amount of coffee the man drank, it was inevitable that he would leave her to use the restroom. He was waiting for him there—hiding inside a stall.

He waited until the trooper was preoccupied at the urinal before he stepped out. The trooper didn't have a chance to pull his gun—to catch more than a shadowy movement in the mirrored wall—before he struck him. Hard. Harder than he'd even struck her.

As the trooper dropped to the tile floor, he dropped the bloodied pipe next to him. He was wearing gloves, so it couldn't be traced back to him. He was careful to leave no evidence behind. Anywhere.

He reached for the buttons on the trooper's uniform. Dressed like the trooper, he would have no trouble getting into her room and finishing the job he'd started. He looked quite official in uniform—every bit the lawman he'd always hated. He grinned at his reflection in the mirrored wall.

The woman was going to be dead soon.

Very soon…

Chapter Six

"Are you sure you're all right?" Dalton asked. He glanced over at the passenger's seat to check on her. He expected to find her eyes closed as she rested or passed out from exhaustion. She had been through so much—had lost so much blood.

But the doctor had assured him that it would be all right to take her out of the hospital. And she had insisted that she was strong enough to be released.

Maybe she was right. She wasn't sleeping or passed out. She leaned forward, straining against her seat belt, as she stared through the windshield. She had studied every street and building between the rural area of lower western Michigan and the urban skyline of Chicago as if trying to recognize it or hoping something might jog her memory.

The bridge rattled beneath the tires of the SUV as Dalton drove over the Chicago Skyway into the city. "Anything familiar?"

She groaned.

"I thought this would be too much for you," he said. "You should have stayed at the hospital with Trooper Littlefield protecting you." The local lawman had been offended when Dalton had asked him to protect an empty room. He thought that Dalton didn't trust him anymore.

That hadn't been the case at all, though.

He was pretty certain that the killer was watching her and waiting for another opportunity to get to her. So Dalton had wanted him to think that she was still at the hospital—still protected.

Instead of alone with just him for protection. But Blaine was on standby. Dalton could call him in or several other agents for backup...if he needed it. But nobody had followed him. He had taken a circuitous route and had kept a vigilant watch on the SUV's rearview mirror. So he was certain they had no tail. But her attacker was the least of his concerns at the moment.

"Are you all right?" he asked. Her skin had grown pale again, making her red hair look even brighter and more vibrant. She had exchanged her hospital gown for clothes that Dalton had bought and sneaked into her room. She wore tan pants and a pale yellow blouse. There were other clothes in a small bag in the backseat, too. It had bothered her that she hadn't been able to buy them herself. But along with her identity, her money and credit cards had been lost, too.

With obvious reluctance, she admitted, "My head is starting to hurt again."

"Should I take you to a hospital?" he asked with alarm, even as he mentally clocked the distance to the closest one.

"No, the headache is my fault," she said. "I think I'm trying too hard to remember—to find something familiar."

His tension eased somewhat. Maybe she wasn't medically in danger. But how about emotionally?

"Have you found anything familiar?" he asked.

"It's *Chicago*," she said. "Doesn't everyone know what Chicago looks like—just like they know what New York looks like? It doesn't necessarily mean that they've ever lived there or even been there. Maybe they just saw it on TV so many times or in movies or described in books that it feels familiar."

"So it does feel familiar to you," he deduced.

She uttered a small groan of frustration. "I just don't know…"

"Close your eyes for a few minutes," he suggested. "Relax." He didn't want her hurting herself.

She must have been exhausted, because she took his advice, but her rest didn't last long. When he pulled into the downtown parking garage, she opened her eyes. "We're here?"

"This is the apartment building where the owner of the Mercedes lives," he said.

"Do you think he could have been the one—" her throat moved as she swallowed convulsively, probably choking on nerves or fear "—that put me in the trunk?"

Dalton reached for her, sliding his arm around her shoulders to offer her comfort. She trembled against him and he tightened his embrace. "Of course not," he said. "I wouldn't have brought you along if I thought he could be the one who had hurt you."

She had thought that all this time and had been willing to confront her attacker? He'd known she was strong, but her fearlessness overwhelmed him.

"Then why did you bring me along?" she asked, peering up at him in the dim light of the parking garage. He'd already turned off the SUV.

"Maybe he will recognize you," he said. "Someone stole his car to abduct you. It could have been a theft of convenience—like his car and you were in the same vicinity."

She looked beyond him to peer around the parking garage. "You think I could have been grabbed here?"

Instead of cowering, she opened the passen-

ger's door and stepped out to confront her fear
or her elusive memories. Dalton jumped out the
driver's door and hurried around to her side of the
car. They hadn't been followed. But if the killer
had figured out that they might come back here…

He didn't want her far from his side in the
dimly lit parking garage. He didn't want to lose
her.

CHILLED FROM THE dampness of the parking garage, she shivered. But maybe it wasn't just the
dampness that had chilled her blood.

Maybe there were memories there—in the
shadows of the steel-and-concrete structure. And
maybe she had buried those memories so deeply
that she couldn't access them anymore. They
were just out of her reach…like Agent Reyes.

He had put his arm around her earlier for comfort and support. But now he stood on the other
side of the elevator. Maybe he was frustrated that
she couldn't remember—that she couldn't help
him solve her case. Before they had stepped onto
the elevator, he had called someone—maybe an
FBI crime scene tech. He had asked them to come
and inspect the garage for blood.

Her blood…

"You have my DNA," she realized. From the
trunk of that stolen car. "Can't you find out who I

am that way?" Jared Bell had mentioned as much the day before.

"We have your DNA," he admitted. "But it doesn't match any on file. Neither do your fingerprints."

She stared down at her hands. She didn't remember being fingerprinted. But then, there was so much she didn't remember. Like that damn ring on her finger...

Claire Stryker was confident it had been there for a while. Why, then, wasn't she married already?

How long had this engagement been?

And where was her fiancé? Why hadn't he reported her missing? Because he couldn't—because he had been with her when she'd been attacked but had been more critically wounded than she had been?

"Was there any other DNA in that trunk I was in?" she asked.

His mouth curved into a faint grin. "From the way your mind works and the questions you ask, I would almost believe you're in law enforcement, too."

Hope burgeoned. She would rather be on the right side of the law than on the side with people who hurt other people.

"But if you were in law enforcement, your

fingerprints would have been on file," he continued and dashed that brief hope.

A bell dinged as the elevator stopped and the doors began to slide open. Panic rushed over her. He had assured her that he wouldn't have brought her along if this could have been the person who'd hurt her. But this person was the link to that car—the car that probably would have been her casket had Agent Reyes not rescued her in time.

He touched her again, his hand squeezing hers as it had so many times before. But this time chills raced over her as her skin tingled in reaction to his touch. His skin was rougher than hers and warm. The man was like that—a little rough around the edges, probably from growing up in a gang as Claire had told her he had, but he was warmhearted.

He cared.

About his cases.

He felt sorry for her. While he felt only pity, she was beginning to feel something more—something completely unfamiliar to her.

"It'll be okay," he assured her. "We'll just see if he recognizes you, if he's seen you around this building before."

As they walked down the hall, she studied the building—the dark wood walls and terrazzo floors. The building was old and dark, but it wasn't run-down. It wasn't even dated. It was fairly ageless.

But the man who opened the door at Agent Reyes's knock wasn't ageless. His body was stooped with arthritis, so that his head barely came to Dalton's chest. His face was heavily lined, his eyes clouded with cataracts.

"Mr. Schultz?" Dalton asked.

The older man nodded. "Who are you? I hope not salesmen. I have no money or time for your pitch." He shuffled back a step as if getting ready to slam shut his door.

Dalton held out his badge. "I'm FBI—Special Agent Reyes," he introduced himself.

"An FBI agent?" the old man asked. He pulled Dalton's badge closer to his face and studied it through narrowed eyes. "Well, I'll be damned." He chuckled. "Tell me what I've done."

"You haven't done anything wrong, Mr. Schultz," Dalton assured the elderly man.

Mr. Schultz chuckled again. "Depending on what kind of day my wife is having, she might tell you differently." He stepped back and gestured for them to step inside his apartment.

She glanced around, hoping to see something familiar. But nothing struck a chord. Like the hallway, his apartment was classic—polished hardwood floors and smooth plaster walls. It

looked familiar in that she could have seen it on
TV or in a movie or even a magazine.

Magazines and photo albums were piled atop
a coffee table. Mr. Schultz gestured them to the
floral sofa behind the table. "Take a seat. Would
you like some coffee or tea?"

Initially unwelcoming, the elderly man now
seemed grateful for company.

"We don't want you to go to any trouble," she
told him.

"No trouble at all," he assured her. "I'm the
chief cook and bottle washer around here." With
that, he waved them down onto the couch before
he disappeared through an arched doorway into
what must have been the kitchen.

"Does he know?" she asked.

Dalton shook his head. "I don't know. He never
reported the car missing."

"Who are you?" a woman asked. She stood in
the doorway of what must have been a bedroom
off the living room. Her hair was white and neatly
combed, her face not quite as heavily lined as her
husband's…if she were Mrs. Schultz.

They both stood as she stepped out of the room
to join them.

"I'm FBI Special Agent Dalton Reyes," he introduced himself but hesitated when he turned
to her.

She hesitated, too. What should she call herself? Jane Doe? Mercedes, as Agent Reyes had suggested with a morbid sense of humor, since that was the kind of car she'd been found in? Mr. Schultz's car.

"You're Sybil," the woman answered for her.

And hope had her heart swelling. "You know who I am?"

The woman laughed. "Of course I do." She reached her arms around her and pulled her into a surprisingly strong embrace despite her fragile build. "You're my daughter..."

Mr. Schultz stepped back into the room, a tray clutched in his gnarled hands. Reyes quickly took the tray from him, but just held it when he realized there was no place to put it on the table.

"I'm sorry," the elderly man said as he tugged the older woman away. "My wife often gets confused."

"So I'm not... Sybil?" she asked.

The old man stared at her with the same pity with which he regarded his wife. "You don't know who you are?"

She shook her head. "I have a concussion that's caused memory loss."

Mr. Schultz offered her a pitying sigh. "And you're so young." He helped his wife into a chair near the couch. "Rose was seventy when she first started having problems remembering..."

She didn't even know how old she was. Possibly late twenties? Maybe thirty? Not much younger than Dalton Reyes, she would bet.

"Does she have Alzheimer's?" Dalton asked quietly as if worried that he might upset Mrs. Schultz. Maybe his edges weren't that rough since he could be sensitive, too.

Mr. Schultz nodded.

"My grandma had it," Dalton said.

"Everyone has someone in their life who's been affected by it," Mr. Schultz said with no self-pity, just resignation. He turned back to her. "But you're too young to be losing your memory. Do the doctors think it will come back?"

She shrugged. "They don't know."

"They don't know nearly enough about the mind." He took the tray from Dalton and found an end table to put it on and then he handed them each a cup of coffee. "And I don't know yet why you're here."

"Did you recently loan your car to someone?" Dalton asked before taking a gulp of the strong black coffee.

She sipped it with a grimace before reaching for the sugar Mr. Schultz handed her.

The older man settled into a chair next to his wife. She'd fallen silent now and withdrawn into her own little world inside what was left of her mind. He patted her hand reassuringly, lovingly, and Mrs. Schultz glanced up at him with confusion and absolutely no recognition.

She didn't even know her husband.

Was her mind the same? Had she passed her apartment and not even recognized it? Had she passed her fiancé and not even recognized him?

"I don't have anyone to loan my car to," Mr. Schultz answered Dalton's question.

"What about Sybil?" she asked. "And her husband or her kids?"

"Sybil died of leukemia in her teens," Mr. Schultz said, "before she even had a serious boyfriend. So no husband. No kids. And she was our only child." Again there was no self-pity in his voice. But there was pain now—pain that seemed fresh even though Sybil must have died many years ago.

"I'm sorry," she said—in unison with Dalton as he expressed his sympathy, as well.

Maybe Mrs. Schultz was better off than her husband. Since she didn't remember her daughter dying, she didn't suffer like Mr. Schultz. The poor man had lost his child, and now he was losing his wife.

"You wouldn't have loaned your car to a neighbor?" Dalton asked. "A friend?"

"No. I have the keys in the kitchen," answered Mr. Schultz, "both sets. I can prove to you that I have the car."

Dalton shook his car. "I have the car—at an FBI garage. It was stolen."

Mr. Schultz shook his head. "No, that's not possible."

"When did you use it last?"

The old man gestured toward his eyes. "Not since my doctor told me I couldn't drive anymore until I get my cataracts removed. So, months..."

The car could have been taken a while ago, and he wouldn't have even noticed.

"And you don't recognize me?" she asked. "You haven't seen me in the building or anywhere?"

He peered through narrowed eyes, studying her face and hair. "I would have remembered a redhead." He shook his head. "No, honey, I'm sorry."

"I know you..." the older woman murmured. "I know you..."

She shivered, uncertain to whom Mrs. Schultz was speaking—her or herself. Would she wind up like that—murmuring to herself—if her memory never returned?

DAMN IT! HE was still furious that he had been duped. He should have known better than to think Agent Reyes would have left the woman to the protection of the inept state trooper. But he hadn't lost much time, because he'd guessed where they were going. Reyes had obviously traced the car back to the owner—in Chicago.

That was *his* city. So it would be even easier for him to take care of them—especially given what he'd learned at the hospital. It hadn't been a total waste of time.

He had managed to eavesdrop on some nurses' conversation. And he'd found out why the only ones coming to see her in the hospital had been law enforcement officers.

She had no idea who she was.

Too bad that she would be dead before she even had a chance to remember…

Chapter Seven

She leaned over the railing, staring at the water below as if she was contemplating jumping into the cold depths. Dalton shouldn't have brought her walking around the city—especially not out here on Navy Pier.

He kept his gaze on her as he stepped away to take a call. His phone had been vibrating in his pocket, but he hadn't dared to take it at the Schultzes' apartment. He'd kept hoping that they would actually recognize her. But with Mrs. Schultz's dementia and Mr. Schultz's cataracts, they probably wouldn't have recognized her even if she had actually been their daughter.

"Agent Reyes," he identified himself to the number who'd kept dialing him. Hopefully, someone else had come up with a lead to the attacker and to her identity since he had come up empty-handed.

"Reyes? This is Agent Bell."

He swallowed a groan. He wanted a lead, but

he would have preferred to get one from someone else—because he suspected Bell's would lead him back to the Bride Butcher serial killer. But at this point, he didn't care; he had to have something to follow because Mr. Schultz had given him nothing. "Do you have something for me?"

"Are you all right? You and the woman?" Bell asked, his voice full of concern.

"Yeah, we're fine." He was only speaking for himself, though. She wasn't fine. She had pushed herself too hard in the hopes of finding something familiar, but those hopes had been dashed. By bringing her along to follow a dead-end lead, he had dashed her hopes of learning her identity. "Why wouldn't we be fine?"

"Someone ambushed Trooper Littlefield in the hospital restroom and stole his uniform."

He cursed. "Is he okay?"

"No."

He cursed again—loud enough that he drew her attention from the water to him. He took a deep breath, controlling his anger. He didn't want to upset her any more than she already was.

So he pitched his voice low and asked, "Is he dead?"

"He's in a medically induced coma," Bell replied. "He took a helluva blow to the head. They're not sure he's going to make it."

"I should drive back to Michigan." He had

brought the state trooper into this case with that damn bulletin he'd put out for leads to his car theft ring.

"No," Bell replied. "Keep her away from here. Keep her safe."

He was afraid that he had already put her at risk just bringing her here. He clicked off his cell and slid it back into his pocket just as she slowly approached him.

Her legs looked shaky; she looked shaky, as if she was totally exhausted. But before he could ask her, she asked him, "Is everything all right?"

He had promised not to keep anything from her. But he wasn't sure she could handle knowing that Trooper Littlefield might not be as lucky as she'd been. He might lose more than his memory.

"No, it's not," he answered her honestly. "We need to leave here. All this walking and trying to remember has been too much for you."

She didn't argue with him, so she must have been exhausted—so exhausted that she swayed on her feet. He reached out and slid his arm around her shoulders—for support and protection. He started walking along the pier, toward the parking area. But she stopped and clutched at his arm. Her fingers were cold against his skin, but still her touch heated his blood.

"I don't want to leave," she said.

"Why?" he asked. "Does this area seem familiar?" He'd already asked her, but he didn't know how amnesia worked. Would something just click in her mind and all of her memories would come rushing back?

She shook her head, tumbling her hair around her shoulders. The setting sun shimmered on the shiny tresses, making the red glow like fire. "No. It's just…"

She sounded so lost that sympathy and concern clutched his heart.

"What is it?" he asked.

She turned her face to his, tears glimmering in her pale gray eyes. "I—I don't want to leave here because…"

Maybe it was because she was so strong that her tears affected him so much—as if she'd crawled inside him, and her pain had become his. He tightened his arm around her and pulled her against his chest.

Her breath tickled his throat when she murmured, "I have no place to go."

SHE CRINGED THINKING of how pathetic she must have sounded. Of everything she had been through, it shouldn't have hit her so hard that she had no place to go. She had been released from the hospital, so she couldn't go back there.

Where else could she go?

She didn't know who she was, let alone where she lived.

Dalton hadn't said anything in reply to her pathetic comment. He had just whisked her out to the parking lot and into his SUV. Then he'd driven her here—to another apartment complex near River North.

"Where are we?" she asked as he led her through the parking garage to an elevator. "Do you have another lead?"

She'd hoped that was what his phone call had been about, but he had seemed too upset for it to have been good news.

"No," he said. "But it's too late and you're too exhausted to do any more running around or driving around. You need to rest."

So why hadn't he brought her to a hotel? Or to a holding cell for protective custody?

"Where are we?" she asked again.

But he didn't answer her. He pressed a button for the twentieth floor. They rode the elevator in silence, the only sound the swoosh of air as the car quickly rose. This building was newer than the Schultzes', or at least it had been recently renovated—probably converted from a warehouse or factory into pricey urban lofts. As they stepped off the elevator, she could see that the ceiling was high and exposed even in the hallway—the boards painted black, the walls all exposed brick.

He stopped at a door and punched in a code, and then the metal door slid open like a barn door along the wall.

He stepped back and gestured her inside in front of him. "We're home," he said.

Hope flickered in her heart and must have shone on her face because he clarified, "My home."

She stepped into his place and stared in awe at the tall windows looking out over the river. Like the hall, it was all exposed brick and timber and metal ductwork.

"How much do FBI agents make?" she murmured. "Maybe I should become one."

With another punch of the console by the door, it slid closed again. And suddenly she felt very isolated and alone with a man she really barely knew.

Sure, he had saved her life. But what else did she know about him?

He had been in a gang. He'd grown up on the streets. Had he really given up that life? Or was he using it to finance his lifestyle?

He looked around him with a strange mix of pride and sadness in his dark eyes. "I have my grandma to thank for this place."

"She lived here?"

"No, we lived in South Side."

"We?"

He nodded. "She raised me…in a tiny little studio apartment above a convenience store. She worked three jobs and barely spent a dime—saving it all for me to go to college someday. I used that money to buy this condo."

"You didn't go to college?"

"I've got my bachelor's in criminal justice," he confirmed, "but my work as a gang informant and a couple scholarships paid for my tuition. I didn't use any of her savings or life insurance money until I bought this place."

Maybe it was because she knew nothing about her own life that she was so interested in his—or maybe it was just that she was interested in him. "When did she die?"

"Before I graduated high school," he said. "She got confused…" His usually grinning face contorted with a grimace of pain. "And she got into it with some gang members…"

Now the pain was in his voice. Like the pounding in her head, she could feel it, too. She reached for him, clutching his hand as he had so often clutched hers to offer comfort and support.

His voice cracked with emotion when he continued, "She died…"

She gasped in horror. "They killed her?"

His head jerked in a sharp nod. "A confused old lady. And they showed her no mercy."

"That's when," she said with sudden realization, "that's when you figured out what was right and what was wrong."

"What?"

"It was something your friend Claire said— that you weren't like Agents Campbell and Stryker, who always knew right from wrong," she explained. "She said that you had to figure it out for yourself."

He shook his head. "No, Grandma taught me right from wrong," he said. "I just hadn't paid any attention to her—I hadn't listened to her—until she was gone."

She didn't realize she was crying until she felt the dampness on her face. "I'm so sorry."

He shrugged off her sympathy. "That was a long time ago."

But like Mr. Schultz, he wasn't over the loss or the pain. For Dalton, it was what motivated him to be such a good agent. That motivation had saved her life.

"Don't cry," he said as he lifted his free hand to her face and wiped away her tears. "Don't cry…"

"I'm sorry," she said again. "I shouldn't be crying —"

"Oh, you should," he said. "You have every right to cry, but for yourself, for everything you've lost. You shouldn't be crying for my loss."

She shrugged. "I don't know what I lost. Maybe I should be happy I don't remember." She glanced down at that ring on her hand—the hand that was holding Dalton's. "Especially if my fiancé is the person who put me in that trunk."

Dalton sighed. "You don't know that."

"Why hasn't he filed a report that I'm missing, then?" she asked.

He spoke slowly, almost reluctantly, when he said, "There could be another reason."

That reluctance had her stomach flipping with dread. "Another reason."

"You already considered it," he reminded her. "That he could have been with you when you were attacked. That was why you asked about other DNA in the trunk."

Maybe it was good that she didn't remember the man—because she couldn't feel the loss that she probably should be feeling.

"You don't think that he just lost his memory, too." What Agent Reyes was saying was so much worse.

"That would be quite a coincidence," he said. "And I don't believe in coincidences."

"Me, neither." She sighed. "At least I don't believe in them now. I don't know what I believed before this."

"I don't think your beliefs would have changed," he said. "You are you—no matter what your name is."

"Sybil," she said.

He drew his dark brows lower over his eyes—confusion etched on his handsome face. "The Schultzes' daughter is dead."

"I don't think they would mind me using her name until you find out what my name is." She wasn't banking on remembering—not anymore. After all, the doctors had said that her memory might never come back. "Because if there are no coincidences, why was I in their car?"

She knew that she really wasn't their daughter. But maybe it had been fate that she would meet them—that she used their daughter's name to keep her memory going since she'd lost her own.

"It must have been stolen by someone who knew they wouldn't notice it missing," he said. "A family member..."

"He said he has no family," she reminded him. Just as she had no family now, either—at least not any family she missed or who missed her.

"Then maybe a neighbor," he suggested. "I have a team already looking into it."

"You will find out who I am," she said. "I believe you."

He sucked in a breath, as if uneasy with her faith in him. Had anyone believed in him since his grandmother?

She doubted he would have brought her back to his condo if he shared it with someone. He had his friends—she'd seen their love for him.

But what about a woman—someone important in his life? Even though he didn't want to marry, he could still share his life with someone.

"But in the meantime, I should call you Sybil?" he asked, his mouth curving into a slight grin.

She nodded and then laughed. "The character Sybil had so many personalities, and I feel like I have none."

"Just like your beliefs, you have your personality," he insisted. "The concussion wouldn't have changed that. You are strong and brave and compassionate."

He had more faith in her than she had in herself at the moment. Gratitude and something else, something even more powerful, flooded her, and she rose on tiptoe and pressed her lips to his.

Feeling like an idiot, she froze, even while her face and body heated with embarrassment. But then his arms came around her, pulling her close, and he kissed her back. His mouth moved over hers, teasing her lips apart, and he deepened the kiss. His tongue slid into her mouth with an intimacy that had her skin tingling.

And passion that she was certain was more powerful than she'd ever felt before overwhelmed her. She wanted him with a hunger that consumed her.

Maybe he felt that passion, too, because he lifted her and carried her from the living room.

Moments later, her back pressed into something soft as he followed her down onto a bed, his mouth still fused to hers—their bodies tangled together.

WHO WAS AGENT Dalton Reyes?

Maybe he wasn't the honorable federal agent he'd thought he was. Reyes would have been told about the trooper by now. Why wasn't he on his way out of Chicago back to that rural hospital in Michigan?

But maybe it was better that Reyes stayed in the city with the woman. It would be easier for him to take them out here—on his home turf.

It had been easier for him to find them—at the old man's apartment building. Of course, he'd known where they were going. And he had caught up with them before they had even left the old couple.

He would have taken them out in the parking garage—if there hadn't also been FBI crime techs crawling all over the structure. Looking for evidence...

Because of the city, it had been easier for him to follow around the SUV. The agent had skills, but he hadn't lost him. He'd followed him back to River North, but he hadn't been able to get into the parking garage of that condo complex.

Of course, if Reyes had taken her to a Bureau

safe house, it wouldn't be easy to get access to her. To them.

He would have to wait until they left. And the moment they did, he would take them both out. Together.

Chapter Eight

Despite the blankets covering her, she shivered. She shouldn't have been cold because, along with the blankets, she wore her clothes, too. So maybe she was cold because she slept alone.

Not that she was actually sleeping. She hadn't been able to sleep since he had left her lying alone and aching on the king-size platform bed to which he had carried her. She had wanted him so much; she couldn't imagine having that desire for anyone else.

And she'd foolishly thought he had shared her desire, that he had wanted her, too. But he had pulled away from her and then, without a word—without so much as a look—he had walked out of the room an hour ago.

"Sybil…"

She shivered again—because the sound of his deep voice had her skin tingling and heating, had her wanting him all over again. Or still…

"You do want me to call you that, right?"

Since when did he care what she wanted? To hold back those petty words from slipping out of her mouth, she bit her bottom lip. So she just nodded.

Sybil was better than Jane or Mercedes. Sybil Schultz was an actual person—someone who had been loved and was still missed. Unlike herself, who, apparently, no one was missing.

"Are you cold?" Dalton asked. "I can get you more blankets."

She didn't want more blankets; she wanted *him*. "You don't have to play host to me," she said. "In fact, you didn't have to bring me back to your home. You could have just dropped me off at a hotel."

"No, I couldn't." He stepped closer and blocked out the light spilling into the bedroom from the hall. "There is someone out there determined to get to you. I won't let that happen."

She shivered again—this time with genuine fear. There was someone out there—someone who had nearly killed her. Someone who had tried killing her again by running an ambulance off the road, by risking other lives than just hers. He wanted her dead that badly that he didn't care about innocent bystanders. He cared only about killing her.

To save face and relieve some of her humiliation, she could have used that as an excuse for kissing Special Agent Reyes, that she'd only done it to get her mind off her situation—about the danger, about the amnesia.

But that would have been a lie. She had kissed Dalton for one reason only—because she'd wanted to. Because she wanted him.

The mattress dipped as he sat down beside her. "That's why I stopped," he murmured, as if he, too, was embarrassed. "It's why I *had* to stop."

With relief, she turned toward him. "You didn't want to stop?"

"God, no," he admitted. "It took all my will-power. But I shouldn't have kissed you. I shouldn't have carried you in here."

Her heart pounded faster with the remembered excitement of being carried in his strong arms—of his kisses. "Why not?"

"Because I can't get distracted," he said. "I have to stay alert. I have to make sure you stay safe."

"So you didn't stop because of this?" She held up her hand. And despite the dim light, the diamond glittered.

He groaned. "No. For one reason or another, your fiancé isn't here." The suspicion was back in his voice. He had pointed out the possibility that her fiancé could be dead, but it didn't sound as if he believed it. "So the only one I'm concerned about is you—about keeping you safe."

She scooted up against the leather headboard so that she sat facing him. "You really take your job seriously."

His dark eyes glittered like her ring had in the dim light. His voice gruff, he murmured, "You're not just a job."

Her heart rate quickened even more, and it was hard to draw a deep breath. "I'm not?"

He uttered a ragged sigh. "You should be. Every other case was just a case…" He shook his head. "But there's something about you—something that's getting to me." He sounded resentful, mad.

Instead of being offended, she smiled.

"I have never lost my head like that before," he said. "I came so close to taking advantage of you. I'm sorry. I am so sorry that I lost control."

"You didn't." She shook her head in disappointment. "You didn't take advantage of me." But she really wished he had.

His handsome face twisted into a grimace of self-disgust. "You were just released from the hospital today. You have a concussion, fracture and amnesia—"

"You're the one who said that wouldn't have changed my beliefs," she reminded him. "Or my personality." It didn't matter what name she was using—her own or someone else's—she had wanted him then.

She continued, "And you didn't lose control." She leaned forward so that her mouth was close to his. "And I'm sorry that you didn't." Because she wanted him yet…

He muttered a curse, and she felt his breath on her face. "You're killing me…"

"Maybe you're the one in danger," she said. And she closed the last fraction of space between them and pressed her lips to his again.

DALTON WAS IN DANGER—more danger than he'd ever been in, even when he had been living on the streets, running with the gang. And secretly informing on all of them.

This woman was more dangerous than any of the bangers he'd known—any of the killers and criminals he had brought to justice. She was more dangerous because she could hurt him more than any of them had been able to hurt him. When he had turned informant, he'd already lost the most important person in his life, so he'd felt he had nothing left to lose.

She was making him think he had something to lose. Like his heart…

And so he had forced himself to pull away from her again. He had forced himself to leave his bed and the tempting woman in it.

Instead of being hurt, the way he had worried he'd previously hurt her, she'd laughed at him.

Then she'd added insult to injury, clucked and called him a chicken as he stepped out of the door. He had stopped and nearly turned back.

But she was right.

He was scared. Of her...

Of what she was making him feel.

He hadn't been completely honest with her and not just about Trooper Littlefield. It did bother him that she was wearing another man's ring; it bothered him that there was someone out there— someone she had loved enough to accept his proposal, to wear his ring...

Maybe that was the person who'd hurt her. Or maybe that person had been hurt with her, trying to protect her. If she was his fiancée, Dalton would have willingly given up his life trying to save hers. Maybe the man he wanted to think was a monster was actually a hero.

So he checked again, but he didn't find a missing persons report yet for a young woman even loosely matching Sybil's description: sexy body, flirtatious smile, fiery-red hair.

He checked hospitals and morgues for a man who may have been hurt with her. Of course, bodies had turned up in Chicago and in surrounding areas. He assigned a team to follow up and see if any of those men had a missing fiancée.

Then he made another call—to Jared Bell.

"It's Reyes," he identified himself when the man answered. "How's Littlefield doing?"

"No change," Bell replied. "How's the woman doing?"

"Sybil," he automatically corrected him.

Bell's gasp of surprise rattled in the phone. "She remembered her name?"

"No," Dalton replied, with concern that she might never remember. She had tried so hard that she had hurt herself. "She didn't like Jane Doe."

"Or Mercedes?" The profiler must have talked to Ash and Claire—probably to see if Ash had managed to talk Dalton into turning the case and the witness over to him.

"No."

"She hasn't remembered anything yet?"

"No," he said again. He didn't bother reminding the other agent that the doctor had warned them that she might never remember. Bell knew the odds of her memory returning. It was why he had been so against Dalton making her any promises.

What if he never learned her real identity?

And why did he care less about returning her to her old life than keeping her safe? Maybe he was being selfish—wanting to keep her to himself. But her life was more important than her memory.

Dalton had to find the person so intent on

killing her that he would even attack a law enforcement officer assigned to protect her.

"What about you?" he asked Bell. "Did you learn anything at the hospital? Was there any security footage with leads to whoever attacked Trooper Littlefield?"

A gasp drew his attention to the doorway of his darkened bedroom. He'd thought she was sleeping. He had hoped she was sleeping.

"This hospital is too small and rural," Bell replied. "It doesn't have any security cameras."

The killer had obviously known that; he was careful. But not so careful that Dalton wouldn't catch him.

"They've never had anything like this happen here before," Bell continued. "The whole place is in an uproar. There's even media here."

"Local?"

Bell chuckled. "Yeah, the pennysaver reporter." But then the humor left his voice as it became gruff with resentment. "But there are national reporters, too." He cursed—probably for personal reasons. The media had crucified him for not catching the Bride Butcher serial killer.

Dalton echoed his curse—because of the danger national news coverage would put Sybil in. Every kook would come out of the woodwork claiming a relationship with her.

"We'll stay away, then," Dalton said with

reluctance and guilt. But he really wanted to see Littlefield; he blamed himself for involving the man and putting him in danger.

"Stay safe," Bell said before clicking off the phone.

Sybil still stood in the shadows of the bedroom doorway. "The trooper was attacked?" she asked, her face starkly white in the dim light. "How badly was he hurt?"

Dalton flinched. He didn't want to tell her. But she stepped forward and gripped his arm.

"How badly?"

"He's in a medically induced coma."

She gasped again—with shock and horror. "He was hit in the head, too?"

He nodded.

"So it was definitely the same person who attacked me?"

They had no evidence of that yet, so he replied, "We don't know that for certain."

"You already told me that you don't believe in coincidences," she reminded him.

He had told her too much about himself—more than he had ever told anyone else.

"You were asking someone about security footage—so he got away again?" Her face had grown even more pale with fear; her voice trembled with it.

That fear broke his heart, so he pulled her

into his arms and embraced her. "It's okay," he assured her. "We're going to catch him."

"You don't know that," she said. "You can't make that promise."

"But—"

She pressed her fingers over his lips. "Bell never caught that serial killer," she reminded him. "Plenty of criminals never get caught."

"But I'm not Bell," he said.

While he respected the other man, he was a different kind of agent. Bell was a profiler; he was all cerebral. Dalton was a street fighter. He had no problem fighting dirty to get things done. And for her, he would fight with everything he had.

So he willingly made her another promise. "I will catch him."

She nodded. But he didn't know if she was agreeing with him or just humoring him. Then she said, "I want to go back."

"Where?" he asked. "Did you remember something?" Because it was only hours ago that she had told him she had no place to go. That was why he had brought her back to his home instead of to some impersonal Bureau safe house.

She sighed. "No. And I am beginning to doubt that I ever will."

He couldn't make her any promises about that. While he intended to find out who she was, he didn't know if she would ever actually remember, herself.

"I want to go back to the hospital," she said.

He cupped her chin and tipped it up to scrutinize her face. Was she in pain and he hadn't noticed?

"Are you hurting?" he asked with alarm. It was good that he'd managed to control his desire for her—no matter how hard it had been. He would have felt horrible if he'd taken advantage of her. "Of course I'll bring you to a hospital."

"Not *a* hospital," she said. "*That* hospital. I want to make sure Trooper Littlefield is all right."

"No." He shook his head. "There are reporters, and the killer could still be hanging around there—waiting for you to come back. You can't."

"I have to," she said. "People are getting hurt because of me. The paramedics, now the trooper."

"They're not getting hurt because of you," he assured her. "They're getting hurt because of the person who's after you."

"Exactly. He's after me, but he doesn't care who he hurts in the process." Her pale gray eyes widened with horror as if she'd had a nightmarish thought. "He's going to hurt you."

Dalton chuckled. "No, he's not."

"You were almost hurt when he ran the ambulance off the road," she reminded him.

He shrugged off her concern. "I was fine," he said. "I didn't even get a scratch."

"Unlike the paramedics."

The driver had a broken arm from getting pinned behind the steering wheel. And the paramedic who'd been in the back with her had cuts and contusions.

"I have to go back," she said. "I have to make sure Trooper Littlefield will be okay." Her beautiful face contorted with a grimace of guilt and regret.

"Why?" he asked. "I've been getting updates about his condition. I'll just keep doing that." And keeping her safe.

She shook her head. "I have to see him." She sighed. "I didn't trust him earlier."

"Why didn't you trust him?" he asked.

"Something about his uniform or how he looked." She shrugged. "I didn't trust him, and now he might not make it. I need to apologize."

"You have nothing to apologize for," he assured her. But he had another question for her. "Why did you trust me?"

"Because you keep saving my life," she said. "You'll keep me safe."

"Yes, I will," he readily agreed. "I will keep you safe *here*."

He wouldn't bring her back. He wouldn't put

her in danger because she had a misplaced sense of guilt. "We are not leaving…"

HE JERKED AWAKE as the SUV exited the parking garage. He knew they would leave—eventually. He just hadn't expected them to leave while the moon was still visible in the slowly lightening sky.

It was just light enough that he could see two shadows behind the tinted glass of the SUV windows. They were both inside that vehicle.

But of course Agent Reyes wouldn't have left her alone and unprotected. He had too big a hero complex. Too bad that complex would prove his downfall. His demise.

His hand shook slightly as he reached for the keys and turned them in the ignition. *This is it.*

He turned his vehicle around and followed them in the light morning traffic.

This was his chance to finish this.

To kill them both…

Chapter Nine

Some might have called it his gut instinct. It had kept him alive when so many of his friends and former associates hadn't survived. Ever since his grandmother died, Dalton had figured it was her voice in his head—her as his guardian angel warning him to watch his back. Instead of his back, though, he'd been watching his rearview mirror.

At a discreet distance, the car had followed them from the city. The luxury all-wheel-drive sedan was a vehicle he would have been following, the way he had followed the Mercedes, if he was still concerned about the car theft ring. It was the least of his problems now.

He glanced to the passenger's seat. Slumped against the leather, Sybil slept now. He didn't want to wake her up; he didn't want to scare her.

But that vehicle had been following them for too long for it to be a coincidence. That wasn't a Bureau vehicle, so it wasn't backup.

That left only one option. Only one person with a reason to follow them…

Sybil's and Littlefield's attacker.

He pressed on the accelerator. The other man had managed to lose him on backcountry roads. But Dalton couldn't be outdriven on pavement.

The closer they came to that hospital in Michigan, the less pavement there was. Maybe that was why the guy had waited and watched instead of closing the distance sooner. He had been waiting for those back roads again. For his chance to run Dalton off into one of those damn suicide ditches…

Or worse yet, this highway wound close to the Lake Michigan shore, with steep shoulders leading down to the rocky beach below. Unlike the way the ambulance had only crumpled a little in the ditch, the SUV would get crushed if it rolled off here.

Dalton gripped the steering wheel in tight fists. If Sybil hadn't been in the vehicle next to him, he would have spun the SUV around and become the pursuer instead of the pursued. Above all the promises he'd made her, he wanted to keep his promise to catch her would-be killer.

He had called in for backup when he'd first noticed the car following them from the city. Fortunately, she had already been sleeping, and deeply enough this time that he hadn't awakened her.

But he didn't see that backup behind him yet. There were no government vehicles on the road, nor were there any helicopters in the sky. He saw only that luxury sedan bearing down on them. So he couldn't confront the killer with the man's almost victim riding along with him.

He couldn't put her in any more danger than she already was. So he pressed harder on the accelerator.

The car thief had stolen the wrong vehicle if he had intended to catch Dalton's SUV. His engine was far more powerful. But he had to slow for a sharp curve as the tires began to skid across gravel. The pavement had given away as the highway ended and became a two-lane gravel road.

A curse slipped through his lips as he fought the wheel, and the sedan gained on him. The front bumper of the car struck the rear of the SUV, spinning it more—spinning it nearly out of Dalton's control.

SYBIL AWOKE WITH a scream as a jolt sent her flying forward toward the dash. But Dalton's arm was there, catching her before she struck her head. He held her back against the seat.

"Hang on," he warned her.

And she instinctively reached for him. But he was pulling away, putting both hands back on the wheel. He steered the SUV into a circle, gravel and dust kicking up from beneath the tires. And then he was bearing down on a car.

"What's going on?" she asked. She braced her hands on the dash now. How long had she been sleeping? Nothing looked familiar to her anymore.

They weren't in Chicago. Because, for some reason, the city had been familiar to her. This area was familiar only in that she knew she had been here since she'd lost her memory. This was the area in which Dalton had found her in the trunk of that car.

Dalton sped up and knocked the front bumper against the rear bumper of the car. The car fishtailed on the gravel, spinning nearly out of control.

"What are you doing?" And then she knew…

Dread filled her, making her stomach churn—making her nauseated. "It's him?"

"I would love to find out," he murmured. But as the car sped up, he slowed down—letting it get away from them.

"Catch him!" she said.

He shook his head. "I can't risk it. Not with you."

"Why?"

"He's probably armed," Dalton said. "If he shot me and then something happened to you…"

He shuddered as if the horror was what would happen to her.

If he shot me...

He said it as though it didn't matter what happened to him, only what happened to her.

But she cared. She cared too much about Dalton Reyes.

"If I wasn't with you, you wouldn't have cared whether or not he was armed," she said.

"Of course not." He tapped his holster. "I'm armed."

"But it's not the Old West," she said. "You can't just have a shoot-out in the street."

"You need to tell the criminals that," he said. "I've had more than my share of shoot-outs in the street."

Of course he had. He had grown up in a gang and then he had joined law enforcement. If he hadn't been shot yet, he would be shot eventually. Maybe he would survive. Maybe he wouldn't.

That was why she cared too much—because she cared about him more than he cared about himself. And eventually he would leave her—whether or not her memory returned.

"That's why I couldn't go after him," he said. "Because you might get caught in the cross fire." The tires hit asphalt again as he drove down a paved road before turning into a parking lot. "And then I would be bringing you here for you—not for Trooper Littlefield."

As he pulled into a parking space, other vehicles pulled into the lot behind him. The sedan he'd struck wasn't among them. These vehicles were all black, like his SUV. He stepped out just as Agent Campbell came around the front of one of those other SUVs.

"You okay?" the blond-haired agent asked him.

Dalton nodded.

"What about you?" Agent Campbell asked as she stepped out.

She nodded. But she wasn't fine. She had already confronted her own mortality, but now she'd confronted Dalton's. Like the paramedics and Trooper Littlefield, her presence had put him in danger.

But he was used to it. He put himself in danger all the time. And that bothered her most.

"Did you catch him?" Dalton asked.

Agent Campbell shook his head. "Found the car abandoned, though."

"Figured he'd ditch it," Dalton said. "I'm sure you'll find it was stolen."

Agent Bell joined them. He hadn't come from one of the SUVs, though. He'd stepped out of the hospital. "You still think this guy is a car thief?"

"He has stolen at least a few cars that we know of," Dalton pointed out. "So, yeah, he's a car thief."

"He's not just a car thief," Bell insisted.

"Nobody's just *one* thing…" She hadn't realized the words had slipped out of her lips until all the agents turned toward her. "What I mean is that no person is just one thing. A woman is a daughter, a mother, a sister, a lawyer or doctor…" Her face heated with embarrassment over how philosophical she sounded.

"So a car thief could also be a killer," Dalton told Jared Bell.

The profiler shrugged. "Too bad you didn't catch him."

Dalton's hand curled into a fist—as if he was tempted to slug the other man. She and Agent Campbell both stepped closer to him—to hold him back if necessary. "I couldn't risk Sybil's safety."

"Then you shouldn't have brought her back here," Agent Bell told him.

Sybil was tempted to slug the man herself. "I insisted. I want to see Trooper Littlefield."

And she had threatened to take a cab or bus to the hospital if Dalton had refused to drive her. Of course, it had been a bluff and one he could have easily called since she had no money for taxi or bus fare.

"He's in the ICU," Agent Bell warned her. "There has been no improvement. He may not regain consciousness."

Trooper Littlefield may not be able to hear her apology, but she still felt the need to make it. She had doubted him, and he might lose his life because of her.

"I want to see him," she insisted.

Bell shrugged. "We'll have to sneak you in the back, then, because reporters are staked out in the lobby."

She nodded. "Of course, a state trooper being attacked would be big news."

"He's not the only news."

"They've found out about her?" Dalton asked, and his voice was gruff with bitterness and dread.

Bell nodded. "They've been asking questions."

"Bet you love that," Dalton murmured.

The other man shook his head. "Let's sneak her in before someone notices us all in the parking lot."

All the FBI vehicles and agents had drawn attention. A couple cameras clicked, bulbs flashing. She felt as if she was dodging paparazzi as Dalton and Agent Bell rushed her into the back entrance of the hospital.

"This is probably the door he came out," Dalton murmured. "Has it been dusted for fingerprints?"

Bell nodded. "It and the pipe he used to hit Littlefield."

"He left it behind?" Dalton asked as they boarded the elevator.

"There were no prints on it," Bell said. "Or on anything else. He's too careful…like someone else…"

The serial killer who had eluded him.

"No," Dalton said. "He's not that careful or he wouldn't have tried to run me off the road again. I could have had him."

If he had been willing to risk her safety…

"Maybe he just had no idea what a crazy driver you are," Agent Campbell teased him.

Dalton glared at his fellow agent, who, like Ash Stryker, was obviously also his friend, as they stepped off the elevator.

Because the trooper was in the ICU, he could have only one visitor at a time. So she stepped into the room alone—well, relatively alone— since all three agents watched her through the glass wall.

Tubes and machines were connected to the bald-headed lawman. He looked old and small lying in the bed. She couldn't believe how uneasy he'd made her before. He was no threat to her.

She had been the threat to him.

"I'm sorry," she murmured. "I'm sorry you got hurt…" And he hadn't even been protecting her. He had only been pretending to protect her.

What about Dalton—who really was saving

her over and over again? What would her attacker do to him?

She knew the answer to her question. She knew that the man would kill Dalton the first chance he got—if only so he could get to her.

HE WAS SO damn mad that rage blinded him. That was probably a good thing since he'd had to rent some fleabag motel room. But it was the only place that wouldn't have wanted a credit card from him.

His cash was beginning to run low, though. He had to end this soon.

Agent Reyes kept getting in his way. The man drove better than any other lawman he knew. But then, he probably hadn't learned to drive on some driving range. He'd learned on the streets.

He could have caught him…if he hadn't slowed down. The man had probably known the other agents were coming. He'd barely slipped out of the car before those other SUVs had driven up.

They'd searched the area, but they hadn't found him. They wouldn't. He knew how to be invisible. He wouldn't have survived prison if he hadn't learned that. Or maybe he'd just gotten lucky.

He couldn't risk going back. He couldn't risk his freedom.

But he couldn't leave this undone, either. He

had to kill the woman. And he wanted to kill the agent.

He knew where they were. So he just had to wait again—until another opportunity presented itself. He wouldn't try to run Agent Reyes off the road again.

His rage dissipating, he could see clearly. The motel room was run-down, the bed lumpy and low to the floor. But in the middle of the mattress lay the gun he'd picked up while he was in the city. Next time he would use that.

Agent Reyes had been able to outrun a car. But he wouldn't be able to outrun a bullet.

Chapter Ten

Dalton hadn't brought her home. Maybe he regretted that he'd brought her to his condo the night before, because he hadn't brought her back.

"So is this one of those safe-house places?" she asked as he closed the cottage door behind them.

It was a small house, but its whitewashed walls and floors made it seem bigger and brighter. Bright furnishings and curtains made it cheerful and welcoming. It reminded her of someplace she'd been before—before she'd lost her memory.

Or maybe it only reminded her of a picture she had seen in a magazine. She couldn't trust her mind—not when so much of it was blank.

"We don't have any safe-house places in this area," he replied. "This is the cottage Ash and Claire rented for their wedding night."

She could see the romance of the cottage—could imagine the dark-haired agent carrying his petite blonde bride over the threshold. Dalton hadn't carried her. He wouldn't even look at her.

He cracked the blinds and peered through them. But he wasn't looking at the view of Lake Michigan. Instead, he was uneasily watching the driveway and the street.

"You have agents out there," she reminded him. "They will watch for him and make sure he doesn't get to us." But he had already gotten to them. He had nearly killed her. She had been lucky to lose just her memory. She could have wound up like Trooper Littlefield, barely alive, or she could have wound up dead.

"I'm not looking just for him," he said. "I'm making sure no reporters followed us, either."

They had ambushed them in the parking lot when they'd left the hospital. More cameras had flashed, and microphones had been shoved in their faces to answer the questions that were hurled at them.

"Who are you?"

"Do you really not know who you are?"

"Were you raped?"

She shuddered at the thought. But that had been one of the first questions she'd asked the doctor who had examined her. She hadn't been violated that way. But she had been violated. She'd been dressed in a wedding dress that she was certain wasn't hers. And she had been shoved into the trunk of a stolen car.

But more than that, her memory had been stolen.

"I don't think any reporters could have followed you," she said.

Nobody could have followed him, given the way he had been driving. If he hadn't told the backup agents where they were staying, she doubted they would have found them, either.

He uttered a ragged sigh and rubbed a hand around the back of his neck. Dark circles rimmed his dark eyes. And she realized how tired he must be.

"You didn't sleep last night," she said.

He shrugged. "You didn't sleep much last night, either."

And not for the reason she'd wanted to be awake—not because they'd been making love. "No, but I slept in the car."

"For just a few hours."

"It's more than you had," she said. "You should lie down for a while. We're safe here. Nobody could have followed you, and we have other agents watching to make sure nobody hurts us. We're safe here."

"Are you trying to convince me or yourself?" he asked.

"I was scared today," she admitted. "Being that close to him...not knowing who he is..."

Could it be the man to whom she was engaged? Could he be that determined to get rid of her that he didn't care who else he hurt in the process?

She shivered. And Dalton stepped close to her, offering her comfort and protection. She wanted more from him. She would lose him eventually. He wouldn't keep her case forever. He would either solve it or pass it over to Agent Bell. Or he would wind up getting hurt like Trooper Littlefield was hurt. Or worse...

She couldn't think about that. She couldn't lose him before she'd had him—before she'd felt as close to him as she could get to another person.

"We'll figure out who he is," he reiterated his promise. "And we'll stop him. He won't hurt you."

"I'm not worried about him," she admitted. "At least not right now."

He touched the spot between her brows, which had furrowed with anxiousness. "What are you worried about, then? The reporters?"

He was. She had seen his anger and concern. Maybe he'd been irritated because all the reporters' questions had led back to one subject—Jared Bell's serial killer.

"They're wrong," she said. "And so's Agent Bell. I don't think a serial killer randomly picked me to attack." It felt more personal than that. Or maybe it was just that it felt personal to her. "For one thing I'm not a bride."

"You're engaged," Dalton said.

"Are you reminding me or yourself?" she wondered.

He leaned down, his mouth coming close to hers before he stopped and whispered, "Both of us…"

"I don't care," she said.

"That's because you don't remember him."

"It's because of you," she said. "You're the man I don't want to forget."

"You won't," he said, his breath tickling her lips. "You won't forget me." Then he kissed her. He really kissed her—with passion and desire every bit as fierce as what she felt for him.

He lifted and carried her again to a bed. Like last time, he followed her down onto the mattress. She clutched at him, holding him to her. She didn't want him changing his mind again—didn't want him regaining control.

So she kissed him passionately, sliding her tongue into his mouth. He chuckled even while he panted for breath. And beneath her palm, she felt his heart racing inside his muscular chest. Then she pulled at his shirt, trying to free the buttons.

But he caught her hands.

"Damn you!" she cursed him as he stood up and stepped back from the bed. "Damn!"

But he just chuckled again. Then he removed his holster and put it and the gun inside it onto the table beside the bed. Next, he pulled off his shirt. And then, his pants. And everything else until he stood gloriously, devastatingly naked and aroused in front of her.

Her hands trembled as she reached for her own clothes, so desperate to remove them that her hands fumbled. But then his hands were there, taking off her shirt and her pants.

His finger flicked over the clasp between the cups of her bra. And the bra came unhooked and fell away from her.

He wasn't laughing anymore. There was no humor in his dark eyes, only desire as he stared at her. Had anyone ever looked at her with such hunger? She doubted it. And she doubted that she had ever felt such hunger herself. She wanted him. So she reached for him, sliding her hands over all his rippling muscles.

And he touched her. Her breath caught in her throat, nearly choking her as sensations overwhelmed her. He caressed her breasts with his hands and then his lips, flicking his tongue over her peaked nipples. She squirmed on the bed as tension wound inside her, begging for release.

"Please…" she found herself begging. "Dalton, please…"

He touched her there, between her legs, where

the pressure was becoming unbearable. While his tongue continued to tease her breasts, he traced his fingers over her mound, teasing the most sensitive part of her.

She bit her lip but couldn't hold in the cry as pleasure rushed through her. But it wasn't enough. It barely took off the edge of her mad desire for him.

His hands shook a little as he reached inside his wallet and pulled out a condom. She took it from his shaking fingers. Tearing the packet open with her teeth, she rolled the latex over the hard, pulsating length of him.

He was so big, so hot—so overwhelming. Then he was between her legs, gently pushing and then thrusting inside her. She arched up, taking him deeper—taking him to the core of her.

They moved in perfect rhythm, as if they'd been doing this for years. As if they had always known each other this intimately…

He knew exactly where to touch her to set her off, his fingers moving over her again. And his lips covered hers, his tongue moving inside her mouth the way he moved inside her body.

She clutched at him, her nails digging into his back and then his butt, as she met his thrusts. And sought release. The tension was like a madness inside her, driving her to the edge of reason.

And then she fell over the edge. She screamed

his name as pleasure overwhelmed and devastated her. He tensed inside her before thrusting deep and joining her in the madness. He groaned, but he didn't call her name.

He didn't know her name. But he didn't even call her Sybil. Maybe because he knew that wasn't her. She wasn't really anyone anymore.

But now she was his.

No matter that she wore another man's ring, her heart belonged to Dalton Reyes.

CURLED AGAINST HIM, she slept again—her small, pale-skinned hand splayed over his chest. Even in the darkness, the diamond glittered and taunted him. It was big. Whoever had given it to her had money.

While Dalton had a nice condo, he didn't have any extra cash. He wouldn't have been able to afford a ring like that. Of course, he could always sell his place. The thought had him tensing with shock. What the hell was he thinking?

Obviously he wasn't or he wouldn't have made love with an injured witness. No, she wasn't a witness. A witness saw something happen to someone else. She hadn't seen anything—at least not that she could remember. She was the victim.

She had been victimized. And now he had taken advantage of her. She had wanted him, but that was because he was the only person she knew now that her mind had been wiped clean.

He had done some bad things in his life—before he'd finally started listening to his grandmother. But those things had felt wrong.

Making love with her hadn't felt wrong. In fact, he couldn't remember anything ever feeling as right. As perfect.

She was perfect.

And by now her face was probably plastered all over the news. Someone would recognize her and come for her. Of course, he had always known that someone was coming for her. The killer and her fiancé. Were they the same person?

Or was her fiancé another victim?

He had checked in with the agents following up on the male bodies that had been found. So far none of the ones identified had a missing fiancée. But that didn't mean that his body couldn't still be out there. In fact, if this killer was as good as Jared Bell believed, that body might never be found.

But, even though no leads had panned out yet, Dalton wouldn't give up. He had made promises to her. He had vowed to catch the man trying to kill her, and he'd vowed to find out who she was.

Tracking down a killer gave him no pause. He'd been doing that since he was a teenager.

But tracking down her identity, giving her back her old life, that gave him pause.

He was reluctant for her memory to return because then she wouldn't be his anymore. He nearly laughed aloud at that crazy thought. She had never been his.

Maybe he was so sleep deprived that his mind was getting messed up. He wasn't like Blaine and Ash. He wasn't going to fall in love with a witness or suspect or a victim. He wasn't going to rush to the altar so he could live happily-ever-after. Even as a kid he'd never believed in fairy tales.

Her hand moved on his chest, caressing his skin. When he looked at her face, her eyes were open—the silvery gray glittering in the faint light like that diamond. Then her hand moved lower, encircling him.

There was no such thing as happily-ever-after. But he could enjoy the happiness of the moment. He could enjoy the woman while he still had her. He reached for her, tugging her up to straddle him.

She gasped as she came down on him, taking him deep inside her. Then she moaned at the sensation.

She was so hot. So tight. So wet and ready for him. He moved in a frenzy, but she came along with him for the ride. She gripped his shoulders and then his arms.

He pulled her head down for his kiss. He teased her lips with his tongue before moving his mouth lower, to tease her nipples too.

She came apart in his arms, screaming his name, as her body exploded around him. He didn't ease up; he kept thrusting until she came again and again.

Then, finally, when he could bear the tension in his body no longer, he joined her in ecstasy. She collapsed onto his chest, her skin damp against his.

"Oh…" she murmured. "That was…"

"Amazing?"

"Overwhelming."

That was how he felt, too. Overwhelmed with emotions he had never felt before. He closed his arms around her, holding her to him.

After the news reports, people would come for her. But he wasn't sure he would be able to let her go.

Ever.

HER FACE TAUNTED him from the television. No matter what station he flipped to, she was there—looking so brave and beautiful in front of the reporters. And that damn agent stood beside her. A muscle twitching along his clenched jaw, Reyes looked irritated.

He was more than irritated. He was furious.

Rage overcame him, blinding him again with its intensity. And he hurled the remote. He wasn't so blind that he missed. It struck the television screen but bounced off onto the threadbare carpet on the floor. The remote broke into little plastic pieces.

But the television, like the woman, was unharmed. She stared at him, her image daring him to finish what he'd started. He would. He always did.

So he lifted the lamp from the table beside the bed and jerked the cord from the wall. Then he hurled that at the television. Both it and the lamp crashed onto the floor. Sparks flew up from the TV as it shorted out and its screen shattered.

She was gone.

And soon both she and Agent Reyes would be gone for good.

Chapter Eleven

"Elizabeth…"

The voice was deep and masculine and familiar. It wound through her, igniting her desire again even though her body ached from making love with him last night. From making love all night.

"Elizabeth…"

While she recognized the voice, she didn't recognize the name.

"Sybil," she murmured sleepily. That was what she'd told him to call her. But even while she'd screamed his name last night, he had never called her anything.

Until now…

She reached out, but her hands only moved over tangled sheets. She was alone in the bed. So she opened her eyes. She was alone in the bedroom, too.

He stood just outside the doorway, as if he didn't trust himself to step back inside the room with her. He'd dressed and armed himself again, his holster lying against the side of his black shirt.

"Why are you calling me that?" she asked. But she knew.

"Because that's your name," he said.

She shook her head. "You don't know that for certain. That must be what someone told you. A reporter?"

"Not a reporter," he cryptically replied. "And I confirmed the identification. I pulled your Illinois driver's license. It's you. Your full name is Elizabeth Ann Schroeder. Nobody calls you Beth or Liz. It's always Elizabeth."

He had talked to someone who knew her better than a reporter would have. She tried hard to think, to summon them, but no memories rushed back. The name was only vaguely familiar to her. She might have once known an Elizabeth.

But was *she* really Elizabeth Schroeder?

And who the hell was Elizabeth? She wanted to ask Dalton a thousand questions, but she was afraid to learn the answers. Maybe it was better she remember on her own—if she ever remembered. But maybe never remembering wasn't a bad thing, either.

"I still prefer Sybil," she said.

"Why?"

"Sybil had people who loved her," she said. "Who still love her." Mrs. Schultz might have forgotten everything and everyone else. But she still remembered her daughter.

"So does Elizabeth," he said.

Her breath caught with alarm. "It was him." She glanced down at the ring someone had put on her hand. "That's who came forward with my identity."

His handsome face grim, Dalton nodded.

"He doesn't love me," she insisted. "Or he would have reported me missing."

She really hoped she wasn't Elizabeth Schroeder because she was afraid the woman was an idiot— that she was engaged to a man who had tried to kill her more than once. Suddenly she had no questions about Elizabeth. She didn't think she was someone she would care to know.

"I'll find out why he didn't," Dalton assured her, "when I question him. I'll have Blaine Campbell protect you while I'm gone—"

She jumped out of the bed—heedless of the fact that she was naked.

He heeded, his gaze ran over her curves the way his hands and mouth had just hours before. Then he turned away. "I'll see you later."

"No," she protested. "I'm going with you." Wherever he was going. "I want to see him."

"He could be the one who hurt you," Dalton warned her. "Who's still trying to kill you. It could be him."

"That's why I want to see him," she said. "I want to know why. I want to know what kind of person I am that he could hate me that much."

He turned back. And this time he touched her with his fingers, sliding the tips along her cheek. "No one could hate you," he assured her. "No one…"

But he didn't know Elizabeth Schroeder any better than she did. So she had to talk to the person who actually knew Elizabeth—her would-be killer.

JUST AS HE'D had no intention of bringing her to the hospital, Dalton had had no intention of bringing her to the local state police post, either. But she sat in the passenger's seat of the SUV.

She wasn't staring out the window as she had on the way to Chicago. She wasn't sleeping, either, as she had on the way back, even though she'd had as little sleep as he'd had the night before.

He didn't regret making love with her. He was glad that he had. Or he might have lost her without ever fully knowing what he was losing.

God, he was a masochist—because maybe it would have been easier if he hadn't known how amazing she was and how amazing they had been together.

But he wouldn't have traded last night for anything—not even for her memories. Would they come rushing back when she saw him?

Would she remember the man trying to hurt her? Maybe it would be enough to put him away for good. Or would she only remember the love she had for her fiancé?

Agent Jared Bell met the SUV as he drove into the parking lot of the small brick building of the police post. "She really can talk you into anything," the other man said. "I can't believe you brought her along."

"Maybe she can identify him as her attacker," he explained. "Isn't that why you're here?"

Because he was hoping to finally close his one open case and apprehend the Bride Butcher.

Jared shook his head. "I already cross-referenced his name against my files."

"Tom Wilson." It sounded like an alias to him. But he'd checked him out—just as he had checked her out.

Bell continued, "Tom Wilson never came up before."

But none of the names in those files had led to an arrest. So maybe it was someone who hadn't come to his attention yet. Dalton kept that observation to himself, though. He'd already been fighting not to lose this case to Jared Bell. He didn't want to just hand it to him.

Nor did he want to hand Elizabeth Schroeder

over to her fiancé. He walked around the front of the battered SUV and reluctantly opened her door. Usually she didn't wait for him to open it. Usually she would have already been out and halfway to the building.

She was reluctant, too.

"You don't have to do this," he told her. "It's not like you remember him."

"But I might," she said, "if I see him again."

That was what worried Dalton.

"But if you don't remember him, you can't believe what he tells you," he said. "Because of the news reports, he knows that you've lost your memory, and he might take advantage of that."

Her mouth curved into a slight smile. "Nobody takes advantage of me."

He had. Several times last night.

Her smile widened, and she shook her head, as if she'd read his mind and disagreed with his thoughts. Then she whispered, "Nobody."

He couldn't argue with her in front of Agent Bell. And he didn't want to argue with her about last night. He wanted to argue with her about walking through those glass doors into the reception area of the police post.

But Agent Bell had walked ahead of them and now held open one of those glass doors.

"You don't have to—" he began.

But she pressed her fingers over his lips as

she'd done before. "I have to," she said. And then she slid her fingers from his lips, along his jaw.

His skin tingled with desire. He had never wanted any woman the way he wanted her. *Elizabeth*...

It was an old-fashioned name, but it was also a strong name. A classy name. It was her.

He saw the confirmation on the man's face as she walked through that door Bell held open for her. The guy rose from the chair he'd been sitting on the edge of, but he didn't rush forward. He didn't reach for her. He just stood there.

The way she just stood there, studying the man. Dalton studied him, too. He was tall with a runner's lean build. His hair was blond—blonder even than Blaine Campbell's. He was handsome in that kind of baby-face, smooth-edges kind of way—an all-American-looking guy. Unlike Dalton, who was a mutt of nationalities.

He felt someone watching him, too, and turned toward Jared Bell. Instead of looking at the reunited couple, Jared was staring at him. He had seen Elizabeth touch his face, and he knew they were more than agent and victim. Dalton expected to see disapproval on the no-nonsense profiler's face; he saw only pity. And something he couldn't quite identify.

He couldn't identify the strange emotions between Elizabeth and her fiancé, either. They just continued to stare at each other. Was he waiting for her to remember? Or was he worried that she would?

"You don't recognize me?" Tom Wilson asked, and his voice cracked slightly with emotion.

Just what emotion?

Hurt?

Or relief?

She shook her head. "I'm sorry…"

"Are you all right?" he asked. "The news reports said you'd been near death when an FBI agent found you in the trunk of a car."

How had the damn reporters gotten so many details about what had happened?

"He found me," she said, and she stepped closer to Dalton as if seeking his protection.

She had it. He wouldn't let anything happen to her.

"Dalton saved my life."

The man's eyes widened with surprise—probably that she had used his first name. Jared Bell's head moved in a fractional nod, as if her familiarity confirmed his suspicions about how close they'd become.

Dalton stepped forward and held out his hand. "Agent Reyes," he introduced himself. He didn't want the man using his first name. "We spoke briefly on the phone."

"You're the one who asked me to come here," Tom Wilson said, and he put his hand in Dalton's.

Like his hair and his clothes, the man's skin was smooth and cold. He seemed more like some plastic doll than a real man. But that was just Dalton's opinion, which was admittedly biased.

The man shook his hand, though, in a surprisingly firm grip. "Thank you," he said, "for saving Elizabeth."

Dalton nodded. He hadn't saved her for this man. "Thank you for coming here. We have some questions for you."

Wilson turned toward his fiancée. "Of course, Elizabeth, I will tell you whatever you want to know."

Dalton shook his head now. "No. When I said *we*, I meant the *Bureau*. I have some questions for you." He took his arm now and led him toward a room off the reception area of the state police post. He turned back toward Jared Bell.

The agent nodded. He would make sure that Elizabeth Schroeder stayed safe. And so would Dalton. He closed the door behind the guy and gestured him toward a chair at the table.

Wilson gazed back at the door, as if he could see Elizabeth through it. "Shouldn't she be in here? So I can tell her about her life, about everything she's forgotten…?"

Dalton dropped onto a chair across from him. "I don't want you anywhere near her," he admitted.

"What!" the man exclaimed as he shot back up from his chair.

Dalton waved him back down and continued, "Until I know for certain that you're not the one trying to kill her."

But even if Wilson wasn't the one who had hurt her, Dalton still didn't want him anywhere near her.

"I would never hurt Elizabeth!" the man hotly denied.

Dalton waited, but Tom Wilson didn't add a profession of love to his denial.

He leaned back in the chair so that he wouldn't reach across the table and throttle the man. "Then why didn't you report her missing?"

Wilson looked away, and his face flushed slightly—either with embarrassment or temper. "I didn't *know* she was missing."

"You don't live together?"

He shook his head. "No."

Dalton ignored the relief that flowed through him and focused on his job. But Elizabeth had already become more than a job to him. "You don't talk every day?"

"No," Wilson admitted. "Elizabeth is very busy. And very independent. Sometimes a week would pass before I would see her or talk to her."

"What do you do, Mr. Wilson?"

"I'm a lawyer, like Elizabeth," he replied. "I also work in corporate law—just for a different company."

"So your jobs keep you busy?"

"Elizabeth has more going on in her life than just her job," Wilson said with a trace of resentment.

"Are you saying that Elizabeth is seeing someone else?"

The guy stared at him, and maybe he was more astute than Dalton had thought, because his eyes narrowed in speculation. "I hadn't thought so…"

He wasn't going to answer any of this man's questions, and it was apparent that he had some questions about Dalton and his fiancée. It was up to Elizabeth to answer those questions—if she wanted. Dalton still had questions he needed answered. "Do you have an alibi for the day I found her in the trunk of that car?"

"According to the news reports, that was three days ago?" Tom asked.

Dalton nodded.

"Then I was out of town. My company had flown me to Miami for a conference." He pulled a plane ticket out of his pocket and set it on the table between them. "I just got back this morning."

Was that alibi a little too convenient? Dalton picked up the ticket, but he also picked up his cell phone. And he called a contact at the airlines who verified that Tom Wilson had been on both flights and none in between.

And there hadn't been enough time between the attacks and his flights for him to have driven the distance back and forth. Dalton ignored his pang of disappointment—especially as the other man wore a smug grin.

"Can I talk to my fiancée now?" he asked.

Dalton wished he could refuse, but this couldn't possibly be the man who'd just tried to run them off the road the day before. And it wasn't as if he was going to let the man be alone with her.

He would have Jared Bell or Blaine Campbell sitting with her for her protection. He couldn't do it. He couldn't watch her reunite with her fiancé—not when he had so many feelings for her himself.

THEY WERE AT the damn state police post. He couldn't get them there. And he hadn't dared to try running Agent Reyes off the road again.

It was too risky.

He slammed the motel room door behind him with such force that the windows rattled. He tossed his keys onto the broken plastic and glass already lying on the floor.

Something buzzed and then vibrated. His phone was ringing again. He knew who was calling—who had kept calling since that damn news report.

He didn't have to play the voice-mail messages to know what they said.

She's supposed to be dead.

I paid you well to kill her.

Sure, he'd been paid well, but not enough to risk his freedom again. This was supposed to have been an easy hit. Thanks to Agent Dalton Reyes, it had been anything but.

He could have walked away. He would probably eventually wish that he had. But he had been hired to do a job. It wasn't personal to him, but it was very personal to the person who'd hired him.

To save his own reputation, he had to kill the woman. But he was going to kill the agent, too. Because that had become personal to him.

Chapter Twelve

The man had come out of the conference room alone. She hadn't seen Dalton again. Maybe he was done with her now that her fiancé was found. Obviously he trusted the man. If he hadn't, he would have arrested him. Or he at least wouldn't let him be alone with her.

Agent Bell stepped inside the room where Dalton had questioned her fiancé, and he closed the door. Except for a couple troopers standing behind a glassed wall, she was essentially alone with a stranger.

"How are you doing?" the man asked. "Should you be out of the hospital yet?"

"The doctor released me," she said.

"But you don't remember anything…"

She shrugged. "Amnesia can't kill me." But maybe it could—if she trusted the wrong person. She wanted to go to Dalton—to have his support and protection.

But she couldn't count on him being around her always. He had other cases. She was just one.

"But the concussion…"

She lifted her hair and flashed him the small bandage. "A few stitches." Or so. "And I'm fine. Really."

He nodded. But she couldn't tell if he was relieved or disappointed.

"Are *we* fine?" she asked.

He nodded again. "Yes, of course we are."

But he hadn't ever tried to reach for her—to embrace her—as Dalton had so many times. Despite the man's good looks, she had no desire for him to touch her. She had no desire for him at all.

"Then why didn't you report me missing?" she asked.

Tom Wilson pushed a hand through his hair, tousling the golden strands. It was pretty hair, but it was the kind that was already thinning. It wasn't thick and soft like Dalton's hair.

"Like I just told the agent, we're busy people," he said as if already weary of repeating himself. She wasn't going to get the answers she needed from him. "I was at a conference in Miami."

So he wasn't the one who had tried to kill her.

"And you were busy," he continued. "You're always busy."

She heard the resentment in his voice. "I am?"

He sighed. "I'm sorry, Elizabeth. I know that you're busy. But we have drifted apart since the baby."

She gasped as shock gripped her. "Baby? We have a baby?" She shook her head. "No, no, no, there's no way I would forget having a baby." She couldn't be that horrible a mother.

"Biologically she isn't yours," he said. "You became her guardian after her parents died."

Her heart clenched with intense pain—a pain she remembered feeling. It was the first real emotion she had recalled. "Her parents?"

"Kenneth and Patricia Cunningham," he said. "You roomed with them in college and during law school. They were your best friends."

Shouldn't he have been her best friend? How the hell had they become engaged?

Laughter tinkled inside her head—a woman's laughter. Then a woman's pain-filled cry as she gripped Elizabeth's hand and the hand of a man. A baby's cry echoed the woman's…

Elizabeth's head began to pound as the memories rushed through her mind like a movie in fast-forward. Panic pressing on her lungs, she struggled to breathe.

"Are you okay?" Tom asked. Instead of stepping forward, though, he looked toward the door of the closed conference room—as if he wanted Dalton to step in and take over for him.

She wanted that, too.

But the memories kept coming…of Kenneth and Patricia and little Lizzie. They had named her Elizabeth.

Tears stung her eyes, burning them. And a sob choked her as pain overwhelmed her. It was like losing them all over again. "Lizzie's alone," she said.

Tom shook his head. "She has a nanny. She's fine."

Elizabeth's gut churned with guilt and fear. "No, a nanny isn't fine. I promised Kenneth and Patricia that if anything happened to them I would take care of her like she was my own."

"You remember?" he asked with shock. "Your memory returned?"

"I remember Kenneth and Patricia." Mostly she remembered the pain of losing them. "I remember my promise to them. I need to honor that promise." To honor her friends.

"You have," Tom assured her. "But you have a job, too. I think you were going back to Chicago to handle something for your office."

He thought? Did he have amnesia, too? Or hadn't he cared where she was or what she was doing?

She must not have cared, either, because she couldn't summon any memories of him. All that filled her mind now was images of a curly-haired baby—giggling and then crying as if her heart was broken.

And it had been broken when her parents died—just as Elizabeth's had broken. All they had now was each other.

"You have to bring me to her," she insisted.

Tom glanced toward that door again.

She could have pounded on the door. Or she could have called out for Dalton. But he didn't know where baby Lizzie was. She knew her friends' home was somewhere near here—somewhere in Michigan. She could envision the house that Patricia had decorated like that little honeymoon cottage Elizabeth had stayed in the night before with Dalton. But she couldn't recall the road or the roads she would need to take to drive there.

Tom had been there. They had been together too long for him not to know. And they had been together too long for him to be a danger to her.

As he'd said, he had been in Miami when the man had tried to kill her. The attacker wasn't him. It couldn't have been him.

"You have to take me to her," she demanded. "I have to see her now."

"She's safe," Jared Bell assured Dalton as the profiler joined him in the conference room where just moments before Tom Wilson had sat across the table from him. "They're talking in the reception area. He's not going to try anything in the middle of a state police post."

The guy was smart enough not to try to hurt her physically. But emotionally, she was vulnerable. With her memory gone, she could believe whatever the man told her. And he could lie to her about their relationship—claim that they were closer than they had obviously been.

He hadn't even noticed her missing.

Dalton couldn't imagine having a woman like Elizabeth Schroeder and not wanting to see her every day or at least talk to her. Tom Wilson might not be a killer, but he was a fool.

"He's not the perp. He's got an ironclad alibi." Dalton sighed. "I'm not sure it's such a good idea letting them talk, though. If he overwhelms her with information..."

"She's a tough lady," Jared said. He carried a thick file under his arm. That was the kind of agent he was—all cerebral, with his research and paperwork.

Dalton followed his gut and instincts and that voice in his head that sounded so much like his grandmother's. His grandma would have loved Elizabeth Schroeder.

"Yeah, she is," Dalton agreed. "She's tough and maybe a little too brave for her own safety."

"You regret her going back to the hospital yesterday to see Trooper Littlefield."

"I regret nearly getting run off the road," he said, "and I regret the reporters ambushing her."

Jared Bell grimaced at the mention of reporters as he dropped onto the chair across from Dalton. "Yeah, but they probably were a necessary evil. We found out who she is. You kept one of your promises to her."

"I'll keep the other," Dalton said. "I'll find out who's trying to kill her—even if I have to turn the case over to you." Maybe that would be for the best—for Elizabeth—if he stepped back entirely. Then she could regain her old memories and her old life without him being a distraction.

Jared arched a dark brow. "What? Why?"

"I thought you'd be happy," Dalton said. "You've been trying to hijack this case from me the minute I found her in that trunk."

Jared shrugged but didn't deny his intentions. "The bridal gown…it seemed connected."

"There are no coincidences," Dalton agreed. And if her fiancé wasn't a viable suspect, then it was even more likely that Jared's serial killer was involved.

But Jared Bell shrugged. "Maybe not accidentally."

"You think someone was trying to copycat the Bride Butcher?"

The profiler nodded. "He would make a good scapegoat."

"But it could really be him," Dalton pointed out. "It hasn't been that long since he killed last. He could have started killing again."

"But why Elizabeth Schroeder?" Jared asked. "Since you gave me her name, I've checked her out." He passed Dalton that thick file across the conference room table.

"She's engaged," Dalton reminded him. He needed no reminders himself. Even last night he hadn't been able to forget that there was someone else out there, someone with a closer tie to Elizabeth than he had.

"But they haven't set a date for their wedding," Jared said.

"How do you know that?"

"Checked out their social media," Jared said. "They've been asked when the big day is and both say they're in no hurry to get to the altar. That they're way too busy to plan a wedding any time soon."

That fit with what Tom Wilson had told him—about why he hadn't noticed she was even missing yet. He'd been at a conference and she was always busy.

Dalton shrugged. "So…"

"So if there's no date set, she wouldn't have

been getting fitted for a wedding dress," Jared pointed out.

"The dress wasn't hers," he agreed. "A bridal shop had reported it stolen the day before I found her in the trunk." Unfortunately they'd had no cameras and had no idea who'd taken the gown.

"Your guy is quite the professional thief," Jared Bell mused. "Cars. Bridal gowns."

"Yeah, he's a pro." Realization struck him like a blow. "He's a hired killer." So it didn't matter that Tom Wilson had an alibi—that oh-so-perfect and prepared alibi. Dalton cursed. "He could have hired someone to kill his fiancée."

"Seems like kind of an extreme way to break an engagement," Jared said.

So extreme that it probably didn't matter that he was inside a state police post. Dalton jumped up, knocking his chair over, and jerked open the door of the conference room.

But he was too late.

The lobby was empty. They were gone.

HE WASN'T GOING BACK. It was a damn state police post. He'd probably killed that trooper, so it was the last place he should be hanging around. But after listening to all those voice mails left for him, he'd gone back.

He had a job to do. And no matter how damn hard it got, he was going to finish it.

When they stepped out of those glass doors, he grinned. This was perfect.

Well, it would be better if she had been leaving with Agent Reyes. But Reyes would have protected her.

This man wouldn't protect her.

He finally had his perfect opportunity. He waited until they got into the rental vehicle and turned out of the parking lot onto the road. Then he pulled out of the gas station from which he'd been watching them. And he began to follow the car. He didn't wait long—the way he had with Agent Reyes, following them for miles.

He waited only until the rental sedan turned off onto a road that wound around an inland lake. The first hairpin turn he sped forward and struck the rear bumper of the sedan. It swerved off the road, hit the deep ditch and rolled.

It was so easy…

He braked. Then he grabbed his gun from the passenger's seat. This time he would make damn certain that Elizabeth Schroeder was really dead.

Chapter Thirteen

Dalton cursed—mostly himself—for taking his gaze off her, even for a few minutes. He shouldn't have trusted anyone else to protect her.

"She must have remembered him," Jared Bell said from the passenger seat of the SUV. "Or else why would she have left with him?"

"Because he forced her," Dalton suggested. "Maybe at gunpoint."

"He wasn't armed," Jared said. "I searched him before you two got to the post."

Dalton sped up. According to the troopers at the post, Elizabeth and the man had left only seconds before he had rushed out of the conference room.

"He could have coerced her another way," he said. "Or tricked her. But where the hell did he take her?" He slowed as he approached a winding road. It reminded him of the one on which he'd found her.

"Down there," Jared shouted. "I see a car

parked off on the shoulder of the road." Then he sighed. "But that's not the rental Wilson was driving."

Dalton saw the car, too. It was another luxury vehicle—a two-seater sports model that would have been much faster than the rental; it would have easily overcome the rental. Dalton jerked the wheel and took the turn nearly on two wheels.

Jared gripped the dash and cursed. "I heard about your driving."

Like his gang days, it was part of his notoriety in the Bureau. Until he had saved Elizabeth with those skills, he hadn't taken much pride in them. Now he hoped he could use them to save her again.

"There's the rental," Jared said.

It lay in the ditch just in front of the parked vehicle. He slammed the SUV into Park and jumped out the driver's door. A shot rang out, followed by the sound of tinkling glass.

He was too late. Too damn late...

He pulled his gun from his holster and hurried around the front of the SUV. Another shot rang out—this one shattering the side window of the SUV.

"Bell?" he yelled, worried that the profiler had been hit.

"I'm okay," Jared yelled back.

Another shot rang out, striking the hood dangerously close to where Dalton stood. The bullet dented and then ricocheted off the metal. He returned fire, shooting at the dark-clothed figure crouched in the ditch beside the turned-over sedan.

Bullets ricocheted off the undercarriage of the car. The man fired back—so many shots that Dalton had to duck low or he would be hit for certain. More shots pinged off the hood and the bumper of the SUV—too close to where he crouched. When he dared to raise his head and look into the ditch again, the man was gone—probably into the woods on the other side of the road.

Dalton hurried down the steep drop-off from the shoulder of the road and approached the car. Heat emanated from the exhaust yet; it hadn't rolled over long ago. And it was still running.

He crouched down, but he couldn't see through the windshield. It had shattered—either from the crash or from the bullet that had bored a hole on the passenger's side. His heart pounded hard and fast against his ribs. He edged around the car to the passenger's side. The window was down and red hair spilled out into the weeds and dirt.

He sucked in a sharp breath—as if someone had slugged him in the gut. "No…" he murmured. "No…"

A few of the tresses moved. Maybe it was just the motion of the wind.

But he called out to her, "Elizabeth? Elizabeth, are you okay?"

Her hair moved, and a hand replaced the red strands—a pale-skinned hand. "Dalton?" Her voice cracked with fear and hope. "Dalton?"

"Yes, I'm here," he said.

"Is he gone?" she asked.

"Yes." He'd gotten away again—which made Dalton feel almost physically ill. But not as ill as he'd been at the thought that he had lost her—really lost her. "Are you okay? Did you get hurt in the crash? Or shot?"

The window eased down more, opening a bigger space. She reached both arms out.

"Are you hurt?" Dalton asked again—before he moved her.

"No," she said. "He missed me. I don't know how...there were so many shots..."

Dalton shuddered. There had been so many shots, but maybe most of those had been at him—since he saw only that one shot through the windshield of the rental sedan. He gently grasped her arms and eased her out the window. Then he lifted her up and held her tightly in his arms.

"Are you okay?" she asked him. "Was he shooting at you, too? Because he turned away and was firing up at the road..."

Agent Bell answered for him as he helped Tom Wilson out the driver's side of the car. "I can't believe Dalton didn't get hit—so many shots came so close."

She shuddered in his arms. "Are you sure you're okay?"

If he had been hit, he might not have noticed it—his adrenaline had been that high because he'd been so worried about her. He almost patted himself down to check for bullet wounds, but her hands were there, trailing over his chest, back and arms. Memories of the night before—of her caressing him—rushed over him. And his heart started pounding madly again.

"I'm okay," he said as he caught her hands and held them in his. At least he would be okay once she stopped touching him. "What about him?" he asked Jared as he held up a shaky Tom Wilson.

"Not a scratch on him," Jared replied with a pointed glance.

He could have set it up—could have had his hired hit man waiting for an opportunity to kill Elizabeth and still make him look innocent.

Anger coursed through Dalton. Through gritted teeth, he murmured, "Yet."

He led Elizabeth around the car, but he took one hand from her to shove Wilson back. "What the hell were you up to?" he demanded to know.

The man blinked and stared up at him as if Dalton had clocked him. "What? What do you mean?"

"I said you could talk to her—not take her out of the police post," he reminded him. "She's in danger—if you damn well haven't figured that out. She could have been killed."

"I could have been killed, too," Wilson pettishly added. And he was still shaking—maybe with shock, maybe with fear.

Dalton was the person he needed to fear. "Doesn't look like you were really in any danger—the shot was fired at her. The killer was trying to get to her." He stepped forward and shoved the man again. "Is that how you planned it?"

"What?" Wilson asked. "Planned what? Are you…"

"Crazy?" The guy didn't have the guts to utter the word. But Dalton had no such problem. He felt a little crazy—with anger at the moment. "I should have known your alibi was too convenient. You hired this guy to do your dirty work for you, and you tricked her into leaving with you to give him the opportunity."

Wilson shook his head. "It wasn't my idea to leave. She insisted."

Dalton felt again as if he'd been sucker punched. He turned to her. "Really?"

"It was my idea to leave," she admitted.

Why? Had she remembered her fiancé and been too embarrassed to face Dalton again?

"Did either of you see the man who ran you

off the road?" Agent Bell asked the question that Dalton should have asked—had he not been so damn angry over nearly losing her.

"I didn't see him," Tom replied. "I must have hit my head when we crashed and blacked out for a minute." He turned toward Elizabeth. "Did you see him?"

She shuddered. "He had a hood pulled over his head, but when he walked up to the car to shoot…" She shuddered again. "I saw his face."

"Did you recognize him?" Tom anxiously asked her.

"I don't recognize *you*," she reminded him. "How would I recognize him?"

"But you remembered Kenneth and Patricia," he said, and that pettiness was in his voice again, along with resentment.

"Who are Kenneth and Patricia?" Dalton asked.

"My friends," she said, and her voice cracked. "My best friends. That's why I had to leave. I have to go to their house."

He understood. They were the only people she actually remembered from her past, so of course she would want to see them immediately. But he needed to see them, too—because they were the only people who could answer all the questions that Jared Bell's thick file couldn't.

They were the only people who could tell him all about Elizabeth Schroeder.

"THANK YOU FOR bringing me here," she told Dalton Reyes. He'd insisted on bringing her to the ER first, but the doctor had confirmed what she'd told him. She was fine. Or she would be once she saw Lizzie. Tom Wilson had had to give him the address because she hadn't been able to, but she recognized the house as he drove the battered SUV up the long driveway to the two-story Victorian farmhouse with the wraparound porch.

A Chicago girl like her, Patricia had always dreamed of raising her family in a house in the country with a wraparound porch. Kenneth had given her that dream. He'd had the house built to look old while being modern and safe for his girls.

Dalton shut off the SUV and turned toward her. "You shouldn't have left with Tom Wilson. You should have asked me to drive you."

Her face flamed with embarrassment over how impulsive she had been. "I know," she said. "I know how much danger I'm in." And if her stalker hadn't driven Wilson off the road as quickly as he had, then he would have followed them right to this house that Kenneth Cunningham had thought so safe. "I'm sorry."

He touched her face, his fingertips skimming

her cheek, and her skin heated even more—with desire. She had met her forgotten fiancé, but Dalton was still the only man she wanted.

"I am not going to let you out of my sight again," he warned her.

Reassured rather than forewarned, she smiled, but then—remembering how close she'd come to getting killed again—her smile slid away. And she released a shaky sigh.

"Thank you," she said, "for saving my life yet again."

"I understand why you were in such a hurry to get here—to talk to people that you actually remember," he said.

"Oh…" He didn't know that Kenneth and Patricia were gone. She would explain that later. Now that she was here, she didn't want to wait another minute before going inside. "There's someone else that I needed to see here," she said as she shoved open the passenger's door and jumped out.

Despite the fact that she was running to the house, Dalton stayed with her every step—ever vigilant of her safety. She was so glad that he was here. That he would protect her and little Lizzie.

She had barely opened the door when the toddler ran to her, squealing and crying with delight. Elizabeth swung the baby up into her arms and clutched her close. "There's my little girl," she murmured. "There you are…"

"Mommmmmma," the child stammered. "Mommmma…"

"Momma?" Dalton repeated the word—his handsome face draining of color with his utter shock.

He thought the child was hers. But since Kenneth's and Patricia's deaths, baby Lizzie had become hers—because she had promised them she would love her goddaughter like her own.

Her eyes stinging with tears, she nodded. "She's my little baby girl!" She pressed kisses against the little girl's pudgy cheeks.

A man stepped into the foyer. Like the little girl, he had curly dark hair. A pang struck her heart over how much he looked like Kenneth. But, along with Patricia, Kenneth was gone.

She was actually relieved that for a few days she had been able to forget the devastating loss of her best friends. But guilt struck her that she had forgotten Lizzie, too.

"I'm so sorry," she murmured to the little girl.

"Was that you on the news?" the man asked. "Were you the one found in the trunk of a car? What the hell's going on, Elizabeth?"

"Yeah," Dalton Reyes murmured. "What the hell's going on, Elizabeth?"

HE PANTED FOR BREATH, his lungs still burning from his run through the woods. He'd had to do that too many times over the past few days. And for a man whose only exercise had been in a small prison yard for years, the physical exertion was too much.

It didn't help that Agent Reyes was as good a shot as he was a driver. His arm burned, blood oozing yet from the bullet hole in his shoulder. The bullet had gone straight through, but the wound kept bleeding. His shirt was saturated.

Hopefully, nobody had noticed him bleeding. And if that pain wasn't bad enough, he had another voice mail from his employer. Another diatribe about how badly he'd messed up.

It wasn't his fault. It was all Agent Dalton Reyes's fault.

But the worst part of that message was that the person wanted to meet with him. He took his gun from his jacket pocket and clutched it close to him. He knew he would need it—not just to kill the woman and the agent.

But to kill the person who had hired him…because he had no doubt that person intended to kill him. This person was more ruthless than anyone he had ever met—in or out of prison.

The only thing he knew for certain was that somebody was going to die tonight.

He hoped like hell it wasn't him.

Chapter Fourteen

Dalton had figured there was a fiancé—either dead or alive and trying to kill her. He hadn't figured that she had a baby. How could she have forgotten a baby?

"I'll explain…what I remember," Elizabeth promised, "after I get her down for her nap." She carried the little girl toward a wide oak staircase leading to the second story.

He nearly reached out to stop her. But a gray-haired woman stepped from behind the curly-haired man and hurried after her. "Miss Elizabeth, I was so worried about you. When you didn't call to check on her, I knew I should have called the police—"

And Dalton stopped that woman instead, pulling her up short with a hand on her arm before she could climb the stairs, too. Elizabeth stared down at the woman with the same expression with which she'd looked at her fiancé—as if she didn't remember her.

"Why didn't you call the police?" he asked. "Why didn't you report her missing?"

"Who are you?" the woman asked, her dark eyes narrowing with suspicion.

"FBI Special Agent Reyes," he introduced himself.

The woman gasped. "Is she still in danger?"

He nodded. "The person who attacked her has not been caught. So, yes, she's still in danger."

"Maybe you shouldn't have come here, Elizabeth," the curly-haired man told her.

She didn't even stop—just kept carrying the now-giggling toddler up the stairs.

"She couldn't stay away from the baby," the woman admonished him.

"Not even for little Lizzie's safety?" the man asked.

"Nobody followed us here," Dalton assured him. "I will make sure they stay safe. But I need to know what the hell's going on."

"She really has amnesia?" the man asked.

He nodded. "Yes, but her memory is beginning to return. She remembered her friends—Kenneth and Patricia. She said they live here."

A little cry slipped through the woman's lips, and the man shook his head. "Not anymore. Kenny and Patricia are dead."

Had Elizabeth remembered that yet?

"What happened to them?" he asked, wondering if it was somehow related to what had happened to her. "Were they murdered?"

The woman jerked her head in a quick nod. "Yes, yes…that is what Elizabeth believes."

The man pushed a hand through his curly hair. "It was a tragedy," he said. "Kenny was my brother, and I just can't understand what happened."

"What happened?" Dalton asked again.

"It was a murder-suicide," the man replied. "He killed her and then himself."

The woman began to cry, tears flowing down her face. "Kenneth loved her. He wouldn't have."

"I think that's why he did," the man said. "So that he would never lose her."

"Patricia wouldn't have left him."

"Why don't you go check on Elizabeth and the baby," he suggested, as if annoyed with the woman's interruptions.

She hesitated, either waiting or maybe hoping for Dalton to stop her again, before she climbed the stairs to wherever Elizabeth had gone.

"Marta and Elizabeth don't want to accept it," he said. "But my brother was an insanely jealous man. He was gone a lot for business. And he'd become certain that Patricia was having an affair."

Dalton was assigned to the organized crime division. He didn't understand crimes of passion— or at least he hadn't until he had been tempted to kill Tom Wilson for putting Elizabeth in danger. "You're his brother?"

"Gregory Cunningham," the man finally introduced himself.

"Did he tell you who he thought the other man was?"

Gregory glanced up toward that ornate staircase, as if wondering if Elizabeth was listening. "Tom Wilson."

"Elizabeth's fiancé?"

"The man had an obvious crush on Patricia."

Dalton's brow furrowed. "But he's engaged to Elizabeth…" No man engaged to her had any reason to look at another woman.

Gregory sighed. "And Elizabeth is…smart and driven. But Patricia…"

"Patricia was magic," Elizabeth said as she descended the stairs to join them. "She was beautiful and loving and loyal. It didn't matter who had a crush on her…"

It didn't appear to matter to her that Tom Wilson might have.

"…she would have never cheated on Kenneth," she said. "And he knew that. He wouldn't have hurt her or himself."

Gregory sighed. "Elizabeth, the police investigated. They ruled it a murder-suicide. You have to accept that. You have to accept that they're gone."

She shook her head, and like Marta, tears

streamed down her face. She had definitely re-membered that her friends were gone, and she was suffering all over again.

"I'll call the investigating officer," Dalton of-fered, because her tears had his gut tightening with dread and his own heart aching with her pain. "I'll just double check."

The guy sighed. "Thank you, Agent Reyes, and thank you for saving Elizabeth. I don't know how little Lizzie could have handled losing an-other person in her life."

"She's not going to lose me," Elizabeth in-sisted. "I'm going to be here for her—just like I promised Patricia and Kenneth that I would be." An earsplitting cry drew away her attention, and she hurried back upstairs to the upset child.

The man sighed again. "That should have proved to her that their deaths were no accident or murder," he said. "They knew they weren't going to be around to raise their little girl, so they made Elizabeth make those promises."

It made sense in that "dying man getting his house in order" way. But how could Patricia have known what Kenneth had planned for them?

"They made Elizabeth her guardian?" He watched the man's face for any sign of resent-ment or anger.

Gregory Cunningham just nodded. "Elizabeth was their best friend. They named their little girl for her." He chuckled. "They always said Lizzie was more like her than either of them—as if the baby actually was her biological child."

He picked his jacket from one of a row of hooks by the door. The hooks were actually crystal doorknobs, though. "I am just a doting uncle."

"You don't live here?"

He shook his head. "Not in this house. But I live in the area, and I work in Grand Rapids."

"So I'll be able to find you if I have more questions?"

The man nodded. "Thank you, Agent Reyes, for saving Elizabeth," he said again. "That little girl can't lose anyone else she loves."

Dalton didn't want to lose Elizabeth, either.

ELIZABETH'S ARM HAD grown numb, but she didn't want to move the little girl. She wanted to hold on to her forever. "I'm sorry," she murmured to the sleeping child.

How could she have forgotten her—even for a moment? How could she have forgotten her promise to Lizzie's parents?

"I'm sorry," a deep voice murmured.

She raised her gaze from the curly-haired child to the man standing in the doorway to the nursery. He was so ruggedly handsome—with his dark hair and muscular body. But his handsome face was etched in a slight grimace. Maybe the so-very-pink princess room that Patricia had created for her daughter made him uncomfortable.

Or maybe it was whatever he'd learned about the investigation into Kenneth's and Patricia's deaths.

"I'm sorry," he said again.

And she grimaced and shook her head. "No..."

"I talked to the investigating officer," he said. "He's certain that it was what it looked like..."

Murder-suicide.

"I don't care what it looked like," she said. "It wasn't what happened."

She had been watching Lizzie that weekend a few months ago so that Kenneth and Patricia could sneak away for a romantic getaway. But then she'd gotten the call that their bodies had been found in their little lakeside cabin.

She shuddered even now, remembering it, and the child stirred against her. She didn't want to wake her. Marta said that she'd slept very little while Elizabeth had been gone. She had left her willingly to return to Chicago to handle a work crisis, but then she hadn't returned.

"I'm sorry," she murmured to the baby.

"I asked Jared Bell to review the case, too," he said.

But she heard it in his voice—the belief that Jared would be wasting his time. So why had Dalton asked him to look into it? Just to humor her?

She didn't care what his motivation was, though. At least someone else would look into what had happened. Maybe they would finally discover the truth.

"Thank you," she said.

His head moved in a slight nod. He looked tired, but then, they hadn't slept that much the night before.

Her face heated as she remembered why. She had been insatiable. And she still wanted him.

"Do you want to lay her down in her bed?" Dalton asked.

She had been sitting with baby Lizzie for hours—so long that the sky had grown dark outside the windows. "My arm fell asleep," she admitted.

"You let the nanny leave," he said.

She nodded. "Marta needed a break." Like Elizabeth, the nanny had relived the tragic loss of Kenneth and Patricia. She had worked for the couple since the baby had been born two years ago, and she had loved them like family. "She'll be back in the morning."

"You should get some sleep," he said. "You must be exhausted." He stepped forward so that he stood over the rocking chair in which she sat with the child.

"Because of last night?" she asked.

A spark flashed in his dark eyes. "Because of

today," he said. "You've been through a lot." He touched her, accidentally, as he lifted the little girl from her arms.

But her skin heated, and desire flashed through her. He gently cradled the child in his muscular arms and carried her toward her crib as if he'd been carrying a baby for years. He looked more comfortable than she had been—in those early days when she had first been granted guardianship of the little girl based on Kenneth and Patricia's will.

"Have all your memories returned?" he asked.

She shrugged, and her shoulder burned as the numbness left her sleeping arm. "I don't know. I still feel like I'm trying to read a book with a lot of pages missing."

"At least some of it's returning," he said.

She sighed. "The part I didn't want to remember," she admitted as she joined him by the crib. "Maybe I forgot on purpose."

"You had a concussion," he reminded her. "I don't think you had a choice."

Guilt clutched at her as she stared down at the sleeping child. "I feel horrible that I forgot about her." The child blurred as tears filled her eyes. "She deserves better than me as a guardian. She deserves her mother and father."

"Forgetting that they're dead won't bring them

back," Dalton said. He slid his arm around her and drew her tightly against him.

Weary and grateful for his support, she leaned heavily on him. "I know."

"Even if Jared finds out that you're right about their deaths, it won't bring them back."

"But it'll clear their names," she said. "It'll take the taint off their love, of their memory for their daughter."

He squeezed her shoulder. "They were right," he said, "to ask you to raise their daughter. You're the perfect person. You're just pretty much perfect."

How could he think that—after getting a glimpse into her real life? She laughed. "You must be exhausted," she teased him. "You're getting delusional."

He chuckled.

And the child stirred at the unfamiliar sound. Kenneth hadn't had a deep voice like Dalton's. Neither did his brother. And she couldn't remember if Tom had ever spent much time around the little girl.

So he wouldn't wake baby Lizzie, she took Dalton's hand and tugged him from the room. Then she closed the door.

"Her baby monitor is wired into intercoms," she explained. "There's one in the kitchen." So she could have brought him downstairs. But it was late and she wasn't hungry…for food. "And in the master bedroom…"

She opened the double doors to the corner room. "I didn't think I would be able to sleep in here," she admitted as she stepped inside the large, airy room with its vaulted ceiling, lightly stained hardwood floors and pale blue walls. "But I had to because of the intercom."

She shook her head in amazement that she had automatically felt so comfortable in this room. She remembered that—she remembered everything about Kenneth and Patricia and baby Lizzie. "And somehow it felt right…"

And for some reason, it felt right that Dalton joined her in that room and closed the doors behind him.

"Like last night," she said, reaching for his hand to pull him farther into the room with her. "Last night felt right."

It was all she managed to say before he pulled her to him again and covered her mouth with his. He was hungry, too; his hunger was in the urgency of his kiss and in his hands as they tugged off her clothes.

She was every bit as anxious, tearing at his buttons and snaps until he was naked with her. But as he had the night before, he put his holster and gun within easy reach of the bed—on one of the end tables. Then he laid her on that feather-soft mattress beneath the wispy canopy. But within seconds he joined her. Then their bodies joined.

She arched up, ready and eager for him, and took him deeply inside her. She clung to him as if he was her anchor in the storm of emotions as her memories returned—along with the danger.

But Dalton brought out more emotions in her, emotions she never remembered feeling before, even though she wore another man's ring. She was falling in love with Special Agent Dalton Reyes. She opened her mouth to tell him, but his lips covered hers before she could utter a word.

Maybe that was for the best. He was unlikely to believe her anyway. He would probably just think that she was grateful that he kept saving her life. And she was grateful.

But she was so much more than grateful. She met each of his thrusts. And she kissed him back with all the passion he aroused in her. She would show him how much she loved him—even though she dare not tell him yet.

She would wait until the killer was caught— as Dalton had promised. And her memory had returned. Then she would tell him—if he was still around. Because once the case was closed, Dalton would have no reason to protect her any longer. If he moved on to the next case, then she would be grateful that she hadn't shared her feelings with him.

Her body tensed, but then he thrust deeper. And ecstasy filled her. He joined her again— with a low groan—as he found his own release.

But he didn't let her go. He wrapped his arms around her and held her tightly against his side— as if he would never let her go. But she worried that he would—as soon as her case was solved.

A DOOR CREAKED, drawing Dalton from his sleep. Elizabeth was curled yet against his side, her cheek on his chest. So it wasn't her moving around the farmhouse. And the little girl was too small to have crawled out of her crib.

Had the nanny returned?

Elizabeth had said that Marta wouldn't come back until morning. The older woman had been upset and had looked exhausted, probably with worry over Elizabeth not checking in. So it probably wasn't Marta moving around downstairs.

He reached for his gun and pulled it from the holster. Elizabeth murmured in protest over his moving away from her. But he had to leave her— to protect her. He shouldn't have been with her at all tonight; he should have been guarding her while she slept—instead of sleeping with her.

Now he hoped he wasn't too late to protect her and the little girl who called her Momma now.

Chapter Fifteen

Elizabeth shivered as her skin chilled. She patted the sheets, but Dalton was gone. Moonlight, shining through the tall windows, illuminated the bedroom enough that she could see his gun was also gone.

Why had he taken the gun? But then he always carried his gun. It didn't mean that he needed it—that he had heard something.

Then she heard something, too. First, creaking, like a door or maybe the stairs. Was it Dalton going down the stairs or someone else coming up?

Marta wouldn't have come back. Elizabeth had implored the older woman to spend time with her daughter and granddaughter and to rest. Marta had promised that she would—and that she wouldn't come back until late the next morning.

So it wasn't Marta.

Was it only Dalton?

She heard a shout—then something else. Something heavy fell over. Something cracked. Something broke.

Dalton was not alone.

He was fighting with someone. Someone had broken into Kenneth and Patricia's home—to kill *her*. Her hands shaking, she grabbed her clothes from the floor and hurriedly dressed. Then she looked around for something she could use as a weapon. Kenneth hadn't believed in firearms, so there were none in the house.

That was what had been so unbelievable about the murder-suicide claim. How could he have shot Patricia and then himself when he hadn't even owned a gun?

Now she wished for one. But it didn't matter whether or not she had a weapon. She had to protect Lizzie. Maybe the best way to do that was by staying away from her. If the killer wanted Elizabeth, he could have her—as long as he left the child alone.

A gunshot rang out, rattling the windows and shaking the floor. A cry slipped through her lips. Had Dalton been shot? Or had he shot the intruder?

She wanted to rush out and check on him. But fear had her frozen to the spot. She couldn't even move when the doorknob began to turn. But then she heard baby Lizzie cry. Maybe the killer was using the baby to draw her out.

It worked. She grabbed a sculpture from the bedside table. The glass dolphin was small yet delicate enough that it had sharp edges. She could use it to stab him—if he got close enough. He wouldn't need to get close to her if he just shot her.

She clutched the sculpture so tightly that the glass cracked inside her palm. Then the doors opened and the man stepped into the room.

In one arm, he clutched the crying child. In his other hand, he clutched a gun.

She screamed. And he stepped closer, and the moonlight washed over his face. His handsome face...

Her breath shuddered out with relief that Dalton was okay.

DALTON WAS FURIOUS. Even more than an hour later, his temper hadn't cooled. How the hell had the guy gotten the jump on him in the dark? He had nearly lost his gun. He had nearly lost his life. And then Elizabeth's would have been lost, too. Maybe even the little girl's.

Lizzie—little Elizabeth.

Her friends had loved her so much that they had named their child after her. And then they'd given her their child. She was so easy to love, though, that he was fighting the feeling himself— as he had fought the man in the dark.

"You should have had backup," Jared Bell said as he surveyed the broken glass and furniture in the formal dining room.

Blaine Campbell had come along, too. Neither of these guys worked cases like this. Jared had ruled out his serial killer as a suspect. And Blaine worked bank robberies.

But then, Dalton didn't work cases like this, either. He worked organized crime. There was nothing organized about the attacks on Elizabeth.

He grimaced over the broken china plates and colored glass. They had even smashed a couple of the oak chairs and toppled over the heavy oak table, they had fought so violently.

As he surveyed the damage, Blaine asked, "Are you okay?"

"No," he said. "I'm pissed. I don't know how the bastard got the jump on me."

"He's a pro," Jared reminded him.

Dalton shrugged. "I'm not so sure. He went for my gun instead of pulling his own."

"What's the point of pulling his if you shot him first?" Blaine pointed out. "That's probably why he went for your weapon."

"We fought over it," Dalton said. That was when the furniture had gotten broken. "I managed to squeeze the trigger."

"You're lucky you didn't get hit," Jared said.

He had taken the risk—to protect Elizabeth and

the child. "I think I hit him…" The guy's breath had whooshed out, as if Dalton had delivered an even harder blow than the ones he'd already hit him with.

His forehead furrowed, Jared looked skeptical. "If he was hurt, how'd he get away?"

"The baby cried—when the shot went off," Dalton said. "We were below her bedroom. I wasn't sure if the bullet hit him or went into the ceiling."

The room bathed in light, he could see no holes in the coffered ceiling.

"So you let him go?" Jared was appalled.

Dalton wanted to hit him. And Blaine must have sensed his intention because he subtly stepped between them and replied for him, "Of course he'd be worried about the child. You'll know when you have a kid of your own."

Jared shuddered. "Not going to happen…"

"That's what I once said, too," Blaine replied. His baby wasn't his own, though. His wife had been pregnant with another man's child when Blaine had saved her from bank robbers. But he loved that baby as if he was his own.

The way Elizabeth loved little Lizzie…

"It's not like I let him go," Dalton defended himself. "The baby crying distracted me for just a second and he wriggled free."

"You didn't chase him?" Jared asked.

"He had to check on the baby," Blaine reminded him.

And Elizabeth. He had wanted to check on Elizabeth and make sure that someone hadn't gotten to her while the other man served to distract him.

"I didn't know for sure if there was only one guy in the house," he explained. "I had to check on Elizabeth and the baby."

Jared finally nodded in approval. "Of course, there could have been two."

"There are two, at least," Dalton reminded him. "The hired killer and the killer who hired him."

A gasp drew his attention to the dining room doorway—to where Elizabeth stood with the baby. She held a hand over the child's ear, as if the little girl would understand what they were saying. Elizabeth's pale gray eyes widened with fear; she understood—how desperately and deceitfully that someone wanted her dead.

"Reyes?" Jared held up a hand smeared with blood. "You did hit him."

Blaine nodded. "We can track him now."

"We may have to wait till daylight," Dalton pointed out. But dawn wasn't far off. The sky was already growing lighter. And so was Dalton's heart. He may have let the guy get away, but he hadn't been unscathed.

How badly had he been hurt? Enough to seek

medical attention? "But in the meantime we can check with the local hospitals and clinics for someone with a GSW."

Blaine nodded. "I'm on it."

"And I'm in the way," Elizabeth murmured as she stepped back out of the dining room.

He should have stayed with the other agents—in the midst of the investigation. But he followed her instead as she climbed the stairs to the oh-so-pink room. He had to make sure that she was really okay.

"You're not in the way," he said.

"Someone obviously thinks so," she said. "Or why would they have hired someone to get rid of me?"

"Now that we know who you are, we can figure out the motive," he explained. "We can find out who's behind these attacks on you."

She flinched. "Maybe I don't want to know."

"We have to know so we can stop him." He touched her face, skimming his fingers across her silky cheek. "And we will stop him." Almost as much as he hated her being in danger, he hated that she was somehow holding herself responsible for that danger—for someone wanting to kill her.

She thought she'd made someone hate her, but he doubted that was possible. She was more likely to make someone love her—even though he had no business falling for her. Not when she wore another man's ring. Not when he'd sworn to himself that he would fall for no one and focus only on his job.

He had to do that now. If Dalton hadn't heard the guy sneaking around downstairs, he might have gotten to her—might have killed them all while they slept. No, Dalton had to stay focused.

THE KILLER NEVER made it to a hospital or a clinic. Dalton found him lying on a blood-soaked mattress in a seedy motel room. Like the dining room, half the furniture in the room had been smashed— along with the TV and a lamp that lay shattered on the threadbare carpet.

"Who is he?" he asked the clerk who had called police because he'd noticed a blood trail leading from the parking lot to the door of this room.

The long-haired young man just blinked at him in confusion. "I don't know."

"How did he sign in when he registered at the desk and got his key?"

"John Smith."

Dalton snorted. "I don't suppose you took a copy of his driver's license or his credit card."

The clerk's face reddened. "He paid cash and signed in as John Smith."

Dalton asked the state troopers who were gathering evidence, "Did you find a wallet?"

One of the troopers shook her head. "No, sir. No cell phone—nothing. It looks like he was robbed."

This wasn't a robbery. Maybe he hadn't carried any of those items on him, not wanting his identity to be discovered. Or maybe someone else had gotten rid of those items for him. "How long will it take the coroner to do an autopsy?"

"We use the county coroner," the young trooper replied. "He has a wide area, so he's pretty busy."

Dalton cursed. "I may need to have a federal coroner do the autopsy. I have to know what bullet killed him."

"What caliber?" she asked.

He shook his head. "What bullet—because it could have been mine." But just because the hired killer was dead didn't mean that Elizabeth was out of danger. Dalton had to find out who had hired the man—which might be easier if he knew who the hell he was. "I also need to get his fingerprints and DNA in AFIS and find out who he is."

"Call the FBI lab," Jared Bell said. He had come along with Dalton, while Blaine had stayed with Elizabeth and the child to protect them.

Maybe it was his bruises from the fight in the dining room or maybe it was being away from Elizabeth and Lizzie, but Dalton physically ached. He hated leaving their protection to anyone but himself—no matter how much he trusted and respected Blaine Campbell.

"We need to put a rush on this." The profiler had admitted to Dalton that he didn't think these attacks were related to his open serial-killer case. But he would want to rule out any possibility that it could be related—that this could be the killer he had sought for so long.

"You don't know this is part of your federal investigation," the young trooper dared to challenge him.

Dalton never had time for jurisdictional games. "This person might be the one who attacked Trooper Littlefield," he said. "I figured you would all want to know that as soon as possible, too."

The young trooper jerked her head in a quick nod. "Of course. Of course, I didn't realize…"

The older trooper, searching the room with her, snorted. "What did you think—we're having a crime wave in this area? Of course it's related. The only other crimes we've had in this area before Agent Reyes found the bride in the trunk was that murder-suicide a few months back."

Dalton's blood chilled. He didn't believe in coincidences. Elizabeth just might be right about her friends. He met Jared Bell's gaze, and the other man nodded. He had his suspicions, too. Elizabeth was insistent that her friends' deaths were murder—just murder—and now someone was trying to murder her. To cover up a crime already committed?

Maybe the attempts on Elizabeth's life had less to do with her than with her friends. The little girl couldn't lose her, the way she had already lost her parents.

Dalton couldn't lose her, either. But he was afraid that he would. Eventually. He would keep her alive and find out who was trying to kill her. But he couldn't keep her from remembering her fiancé and returning to him. Unless Tom Wilson was the person who'd hired the hit man.

Chapter Sixteen

Pain radiated throughout Elizabeth's head, blurring her vision. It was as if she had been struck all over again. The throbbing was intense, echoing inside her skull. Was it because of the concussion?

Or was it because her memory was returning? Because along with those memories came pain. It was like losing Kenneth and Patricia all over again.

Or was it because she'd had another sleepless night? Because she was falling in love with a man who wouldn't stay? Since the break-in, she hadn't seen him. Shortly after talking to her, he had left the house with Jared Bell—leaving Blaine Campbell to protect her.

"Are you okay?" Agent Campbell asked as he jostled the little girl on his lean hip. Baby Lizzie giggled now. She'd been crying earlier—tired and cranky from having her sleep disrupted.

Maybe that was why Elizabeth's head was

pounding. She had been rocking the little girl in the nursery, but it had only intensified her pain and little Lizzie's crying. So she held the rocking chair still while Agent Campbell held the toddler.

"I'll be okay," she replied. When Dalton returned.

If Dalton returned.

"Thank you," she added. "Not just for protecting me but for helping with the baby."

"I'm happy to help out," he said. "Keeping you safe and helping with this little princess." He'd switched the bouncing to rocking in his arms, and now Lizzie's curly-haired head bobbed as she fell asleep.

"You're a natural," she said.

"My wife and I have a son," he shared with a father's pride.

She remembered Dalton's horror over being mistaken for a groom. He probably felt the same way about fatherhood as he did marriage. He was probably just as averse. But she understood that he was devoted to his job—to avenge the loss of his grandmother and to make her proud.

"He's only eight weeks old," Blaine continued, "so quite a bit smaller than this young lady. But with the way he eats, I'm sure he'll catch up soon."

"They grow up fast," Elizabeth said. She'd been gone less than a week, but the curly-haired toddler seemed so much bigger to her. So much older. She was growing up so fast. How soon before she forgot her parents?

She had already started calling Elizabeth Momma. She had replaced Patricia in her mind. But Elizabeth would make sure that the little girl always knew who her real mother was. She would keep their memories alive for Kenneth and Patricia. But she could only do that if she were still alive.

A door creaked—reminding her of the noises that had awakened her the night before. Then the stairs creaked as someone began to climb them. There was another intruder in the house. Agent Campbell passed her the toddler as he pulled his gun from his holster.

"It's me," a deep voice called out.

The sleepy girl lifted her head from Elizabeth's shoulder. She already recognized Dalton's voice. Her face brightened, and she smiled at him as he stepped inside the nursery.

Elizabeth wanted to smile, too, but she held her breath instead. He had left the house for a reason—to follow a lead. "What was it?" she asked. "Did you find him?"

He pulled his phone from his pocket and turned the screen toward her, displaying the picture of a man's face. His eyes were closed, his face ashen.

She gasped. "He's dead?"

"Yes."

"Are you all right?" she asked. "Was there another struggle?"

He shook his head. "No, the hotel clerk found him dead in his room. I think he might be who I struggled with last night."

But his deep voice held a hint of doubt.

Blaine must have picked up on it, too, because he asked, "You're not certain?"

Dalton shrugged. "I thought he was bigger. Taller. Broader." He sighed. "But it was late. And I was tired."

Which was her fault. She had kept him awake two nights in a row—making love.

"Do you recognize him?" he asked her.

"I wasn't down here when you struggled with him," she reminded him. Embarrassment heated her face. She had been upstairs in her room—frozen with fear—unable to help him or herself.

"I don't mean from last night," he said and clarified his earlier question by adding, "Do you recognize him at all?"

She shrugged now. "I don't know. I remember some things." Like little Lizzie and Kenneth and Patricia and the house. But she didn't remember her own fiancé. "But there's so much I don't remember."

"Could he be the man who shot at you after he ran you and Wilson off the road?"

"I was upside down." Her head pressed against the roof of the car. "And he had his hood pulled tight around his face," she said. "It could be him." She peered closer at the screen. "But I'm not sure."

"It's okay," Agent Campbell said. He offered her assurance, while she felt Dalton's frustration.

Was he upset with her? With her inability to help at all? He wasn't the only one; she was frustrated, too. She wanted her memories back—all of them. She wanted her life back, and the danger gone.

But she knew if that happened, Dalton would be gone, too.

"I got some other news on the way over here," Dalton said. "Trooper Littlefield's out of the coma."

"That's great news!" Agent Campbell exclaimed. "He's a nice guy and a really good trooper."

A memory flashed into Elizabeth's mind—of the uniform and her resentment of it. "He investigated Kenneth's and Patricia's murders," she said as the memory became clearer. "I talked to him before."

While she was relieved that he was all right now, she understood why she had been suspicious and resentful of him even when she hadn't remembered him. "He didn't listen to me, though. He didn't look deeper into their deaths."

Dalton shook his head. "I spoke to the officer in charge of the investigation. It wasn't Trooper Littlefield."

"There were two of them," she conceded. "An older officer and Trooper Littlefield. I talked to both of them. But neither of them listened to me."

"You remember all that?" Agent Campbell asked skeptically. He looked at her with suspicion now, as if he wondered if she had faked the amnesia.

She sighed. "Yes. I remember—like I remember little Lizzie."

"But you don't remember Tom Wilson," Dalton reminded her.

She shrugged. "I don't know why. Maybe I remember Kenneth and Patricia so clearly because I'm so upset about the injustice. Nobody listened to me then about their deaths and nobody's listening now." Frustration overwhelmed her, and tears stung her eyes and nose. "Their names will never be cleared, their real killer never found."

"I'm listening," Dalton assured her. Over the little girl's head, his dark gaze held hers. "And I'll talk to Littlefield about the investigation."

She snorted in derision. "What investigation? There really wasn't one."

"There will be now," Dalton said. He turned toward his friend. "Can you stay for a while longer?"

Blaine nodded. "Yes, but I want to talk to you

before you leave." The other agent stepped outside the room.

Dalton didn't follow him right away. Instead, he stepped closer to her and reached out a hand. He patted little Lizzie's curly head and skimmed a finger along her cheek. "She's asleep. I hope last night wasn't too traumatic for her." But as he said it, he watched Elizabeth's face.

She didn't know if he was referring to the break-in or to her falling in love with him. Did he know how she felt about him? Did it show on her face? Her love? Her longing?

"She's been through a lot," Elizabeth replied.

"I know," he said. And again, she thought he was referring to her and not the child. "Too much."

"Do you know who he is?" she asked. "The man found in the motel?"

"A recently paroled former car thief," Dalton said. "His prints were on file. Ronnie Hoover worked as a parking attendant in the garage where Mr. Schultz kept his car."

"The building looked familiar to me," she said. "I may have an apartment there, too." But she remembered this house better. "That might be how he grabbed me."

"You think he could just be a random stalker?" he asked.

"Clearly, you don't think so," she said as she heard the doubt in his voice.

He shrugged. "You could have picked up a random stalker. But I don't think you've even spent that much time in Chicago since becoming little Elizabeth's guardian."

She shook her head. "No, I don't think so, either—not from what I remember and not from what Marta said. So you don't think this is random?"

"No. But I will figure it out." He made her another promise.

But all the promises he'd made had been about her memory and her attacker, about giving her life back to her—not about sharing it. Once he figured everything out, he would leave. Just as he turned to leave now.

But before he walked out into the hall to join his friend, he leaned down and he brushed a soft kiss across her mouth. Her heart shifted, swelling with the love she felt for him. A love she doubted that he would ever return…

WHY HADN'T TROOPER LITTLEFIELD identified her? When Dalton had found her in the trunk, the trooper had acted as if he'd never seen her before. But Littlefield had seen her; he had argued with her, if Dalton knew Elizabeth at all.

And Dalton knew Elizabeth.

She was strong. And stubborn and determined to prove that her friend hadn't killed his wife and then himself. The lawyer in her—even though her specialty was corporate law—would have had her arguing her case, proving her point.

She would have been memorable. Dalton knew that he would never forget her. And probably never get over her.

He drew in a deep breath as the thought jabbed his ribs with a twinge of pain.

"You okay?" Trooper Littlefield asked him as he opened his eyes and focused on Dalton's face.

Dalton chuckled. "You're the one just coming out of a coma," he said. Actually, he'd worried the man might have slipped back into it when he'd stepped into his hospital room and found him asleep. "Are you okay?"

The trooper lifted a hand to his heavily bandaged head. "Good thing it was already shaved, huh? I don't have to worry about my hair."

"No, you don't," Dalton agreed.

The man's pale face flushed with color. "I'm sorry," he said. "I screwed up, letting the guy get the jump on me again—like when he stole my car."

Dalton had thought it odd that the trooper had left his car down the block. Had that been a mistake or something else? But if the trooper had had some type of arrangement with the paroled car thief, why had he called Dalton to the scene at all?

"It's a good thing you didn't trust me to protect her," the trooper added.

"I trusted you," Dalton said. Then.

"You were right," Littlefield continued, "that he was waiting for another opportunity to get to her."

"He got to you instead," Dalton said. "You're lucky to be alive." And if Littlefield and Ronnie Hoover had been working together, why had the criminal turned on him? Not that that hadn't happened before. According to the old friends Dalton had put away, he had turned on them.

Littlefield shuddered. "The doctors are amazed that I came out of the coma."

"Is your memory intact?" Dalton asked.

"Yes," Littlefield replied. "I'll be able to identify the bastard, too. I saw his face in the mirror right before he hit me."

Dalton held out his phone with the picture displayed.

Littlefield's breath escaped in a shocked gasp. "He's dead?"

Dalton nodded.

"Yeah, that's him," he replied. "What happened to him?"

"I'm still waiting to hear from the Bureau coroner," he replied. He didn't know for certain that his bullet had killed the man.

Littlefield nodded. "That's good that you're not

relying on Doc Brouwer. He's stretched too thin, as it is."

"Is he the one who investigated the deaths of Kenneth and Patricia Cunningham?"

Littlefield tensed and cursed. "That's who she is. The amnesia victim—she's related to those people. I remember her now."

"Elizabeth Schroeder," Dalton said. "She's a corporate lawyer from Chicago." And the guardian of a small child and someone's fiancée. As she'd already pointed out, no person was just one thing. But Dalton. He was only an FBI special agent. "We already learned her identity."

"Her memory returned?"

Not all of it. But he nodded. "She definitely remembers her friends."

"She doesn't believe it was a murder-suicide," Littlefield recalled.

"Do you?" Dalton asked.

The trooper hesitated just long enough that Dalton realized he had doubts, too. "Trooper Jackson was the senior investigator. He believed it was a murder-suicide."

"She said that he wouldn't listen to her," Dalton said. "She said that neither would you."

Littlefield sighed. "I think she's right that it didn't happen exactly the way the report reads."

"You don't think so?"

He shook his heavily bandaged head and flinched. "I think that the husband died first."

"You think the wife killed him and then herself?"

Littlefield nodded—but just slightly. "It looked that way. Doc thought he was dead longer. And his blood was under hers on the gun."

"Meaning she died last." Dalton had seen the crime-scene photos. "But the gun was in his hand…" The scene had been staged.

Littlefield groaned. "You think she's right. That the couple was murdered?"

"I think that it's an odd coincidence that Elizabeth is the only one fighting to keep the investigation open, to prove that her friends were murdered, and then she is nearly murdered."

"You think whoever killed them has been trying to kill her?" He pointed toward Dalton's phone. "Do you think it was him?"

Dalton shook his head. "It couldn't be. He was in prison when they were murdered." So if Kenneth and Patricia had been murdered—as he was beginning to believe—then their killer was still out there.

Littlefield grimaced again, but he hadn't moved his head at all. "Maybe I need to rethink my career," he murmured. "I may not be cut out for this job."

Dalton wanted to argue with him, but he was

beginning to feel the way Elizabeth felt. Outraged that there had been no justice for her friends yet.

"Get some rest," Dalton suggested. "You'll feel better." He wouldn't feel better until he knew for certain who was trying to kill Elizabeth.

His cell vibrated in his pocket. He didn't click the talk button until he had stepped out of the trooper's room and into the hall. "Reyes here."

"You put a bullet in this guy," Jared Bell said. "But it wasn't what killed him."

"It wasn't?" There had been so much blood.

"That was the knife wound."

"I didn't have a knife in the dining room," Dalton said.

"He was dead before then," Jared added. "You must have shot him when he ran Elizabeth and her fiancé off the road earlier that day. I would bet whoever hired him killed him."

"And then broke into Elizabeth's house to finish the job he had paid Ronnie Hoover to do," Dalton said. "Are you with her?"

"No," Jared replied. "I'm still at the coroner's."

"Blaine had to leave early." That was why he'd called Dalton into the hall—to tell him that he couldn't stay much longer to protect her.

"There are guards all around the place," Jared assured him. "Nobody's getting inside to her."

Dalton wasn't that convinced. The only thing he knew for certain was that he had left Elizabeth and Lizzie alone. And that the person who really wanted her dead was still alive and determined to finish the job.

HER HAND SHAKING, Elizabeth wrapped it around the knob and drew the door open to face her fiancé.

"Thanks for agreeing to see me," Tom Wilson said as he stepped inside and closed the door behind him—shutting out the lawmen who were supposed to protect her.

She wasn't certain she had done the right thing. Maybe she shouldn't have let him past the young FBI agent and the trooper guarding the outside of the house. Maybe she shouldn't have let him inside with her—because, according to Dalton, she was still in danger. The man he had found dead had probably only been doing what he'd been paid to do. What someone else had paid him to do.

Tom Wilson, with his perfect hair, face and clothes, looked like the kind of man who would hire someone else to do his dirty work. But why would he want to hurt her?

To kill her?

Why not just ask for his ring back instead of trying to permanently get rid of her? Unless he had another reason, unless he had done something else—something horrible...

Had he really had a crush on Patricia? She'd

been so beautiful with her long blond hair and bright blue eyes. But her inner beauty had been even more captivating. She'd been loving and loyal. She had never looked at any man but Kenneth. She wouldn't have left him for anyone. Tom would have known that he could never have her. And if he couldn't have her, had he not wanted anyone else to?

Tom was looking at her strangely, as if he was worried that she didn't remember him yet. Or maybe he was more worried that she did remember him.

And maybe what he'd done to her…

And to Kenneth and Patricia…

Before she could say anything, he reached for her. His hands closing roughly around her shoulders, he jerked her to him.

Chapter Seventeen

A sense of foreboding and urgency drove Dalton back to Elizabeth's house. He pressed the accelerator to the floor, risking the speed on the dark and unfamiliar roads—because he would risk anything for Elizabeth, to keep her safe.

He had promised to protect her, but he'd left her unprotected. Sure, there were guards outside—a lower-level agent and a local trooper or deputy. That wasn't protection in which Dalton had much confidence. Growing up the way he had, he didn't trust easily. So he only had a few true friends.

And two of those were gone on their honeymoon. Maybe he should have asked them to stay.

The lights of the house twinkled in the distance—at the end of the winding driveway leading up to it. He slammed on his brakes at the squad car that blocked the entrance. He put down the window and flashed his badge at the trooper.

"Special Agent Reyes," the man said as he read

Dalton's shield. "You were going to see Little-field. How is he?"

"Fine," he replied shortly. "Did you let anyone go up to the house tonight?"

The guy tensed—hopefully, just with irritation at Dalton's curtness. But then he replied, "We let her fiancé through."

"When?" Dalton asked.

"Just a little while ago."

"Move your damn car," he ordered as fear gripped him. He didn't trust Tom Wilson, and it wouldn't take the man long to finish the job he'd hired someone else to do. The car had barely backed up when he squeezed his SUV between it and the fence. Then he pressed hard on the accelerator and raced up to the house.

He slammed it into Park and jumped out while it was still moving. Drawing his gun from his holster, he leaped up the steps to the porch and threw open the front door. Little Lizzie's cries drifted down from upstairs, drawing his concern. Elizabeth would have never let her cry.

Then he heard the struggle—something falling. And he turned toward the front room—where the man held Elizabeth tightly while she pounded her fists on his back and shoulders. She was a fighter.

Rage rushed over him, heating his blood and

making his heart race. "Get your damn hands off her!" he shouted. Instead of cocking his gun, he holstered it and reached for the man, jerking him away from her. Then, like Elizabeth, he used his fists. Instead of pounding on his back, though, he pounded on his face—shoving his fist right into Tom Wilson's jaw. Wilson dropped to the floor with a heavy thud.

And Elizabeth dropped to her knees beside him. "Oh, my God, are you all right?" She glanced up at Dalton and glared at him. "Why did you hit him?"

"You were hitting him," he said. "He was hurting you."

She shook her head. "No. He wasn't hurting me." She sighed. "I was hurting him…"

Dalton narrowed his eyes. "What? He was all over you." Then he realized why and wished he'd hit him harder.

Wilson groaned, though, and shifted around on the floor as he regained consciousness.

Elizabeth glanced up again, but higher—toward the ceiling. "Would you go upstairs and check on Lizzie?"

Dalton hesitated. He didn't want to leave her alone to be mauled again by another man—even though that man was her fiancé. "If he tries to touch you…"

He would hit him harder. He didn't care that

Wilson was her real fiancé. Dalton felt as though she was his. That feeling of possessiveness overwhelmed and chilled him. He had never felt that way before. But then, Elizabeth Schroeder made him feel a lot of things he had never felt before.

He gave Tom Wilson his most menacing glare before he headed up the stairs to the little girl. He opened the door and stepped inside the pink room. The tiny princess stood in her crib. Her hands gripped the top of the railing as if she was ready to climb out.

He didn't give her long before she figured out how. His granny had always said that there wasn't a crib created that could have held him.

Her chocolate-brown curls were damp and stuck to her face, which was red and flushed from her tears. But the minute she saw him, her tears stopped and her little grimace turned into a smile. And something shifted inside his chest, squeezing his heart. He wasn't just falling for Elizabeth. He was falling for her goddaughter, too.

"Come here, baby," he said as he reached inside the crib for her.

She gripped his arms and clung to him. When he lifted her up, she settled her head beneath his chin and sighed. He rubbed her back. "It's all right, sweetheart. It's all right."

But it wasn't. He didn't like leaving Elizabeth alone with Tom Wilson—even if the man posed no physical threat to her. He posed a threat to Dalton. Wilson was her fiancé. Dalton was just her protector.

And he worried that he wasn't doing a very good job of protecting her by leaving her alone with a man she didn't even remember. He could have been abusive to her. He could have been a danger…

ELIZABETH'S PULSE SETTLED back down to an even pace as the little girl's cries subsided. Dalton had her now. He was taking care of little Lizzie—the way he tried to take care of her.

Tom groaned and sat up. His hand rubbed his jaw, which he moved back and forth as if testing to see if it was broken. Had Dalton broken it? He'd certainly hit him hard enough.

"What the hell's wrong with that agent?" Tom asked, his chest puffing out with righteous indignation.

"What the hell's wrong with you?" Elizabeth asked, and she slapped his already bruised face.

He groaned again and flinched.

"You can't just grab me and try to force yourself on me," she said, and her pulse quickened again with the fear she'd felt as she had tried to fight him off.

"I was trying to get you to remember me," he admitted. "You remember everyone else but me."

Had that really hurt him—as she'd told Dalton she had? Or was it only wounded pride that had brought him here to try to jar her memory?

"I'm your fiancé," he said. "We've been engaged for two years. We dated three years before that. How could you just forget me?"

"I forgot everything," she reminded him. "My amnesia was complete. I didn't even remember my own name. I didn't remember *myself*." But she hadn't felt any differently then than she did now. Dalton had been right—that her character and her values hadn't changed.

"But you remember all of that now," he said, his voice wavering with a faint whine. "You remember everything and everyone but *me*."

"I remember," she said. But with none of the intense emotion that she had remembered Kenneth and Patricia and baby Lizzie...

"You do?" he asked with skepticism and nerves apparent in his voice.

Did he really want her to remember?

It was too late—if he had changed his mind. His kiss hadn't brought the memories back, but when Dalton had hit him so hard that he'd knocked him out, she had cared. She hadn't wanted him hurt.

"We have known each other a long time," she said.

He smiled then winced and touched his swollen jaw. "Yes, we have."

"We've been engaged for two years," she said, even though she wasn't certain it was actually that long. She couldn't remember exactly when he'd proposed—the night had felt like any other dinner date.

"Yes."

"We don't live together," she said.

He shook his head, and his brow furrowed slightly as if he was growing concerned about her memories.

He had reason to be concerned.

"We haven't set a date for our wedding," she said.

"We've been busy," he said, "especially since Kenneth and Patricia died. You've been dividing your time between Chicago and here—between me and Lizzie."

"Why?" she asked.

His brow furrowed more. "What do you mean?"

"Why haven't we set a date?"

"I just told you—"

"Kenneth and Patricia died a few months ago," she said. "We were engaged over a year before that. Usually the first thing couples do when they get engaged is set a date—because they're anxious to get married." The way Kenneth and Patricia had been. Apparently, Dalton's friends Ash and Claire had also been anxious and ecstatically in love.

"We're not that kind of people," he said. "We don't rush into anything."

"Then why don't we at least live together?" she asked. "Especially now. Why aren't you helping me with little Lizzie?"

He sighed—a churlish sigh of irritation. "*You* are her guardian. Not *me*."

And why was that? Hadn't Kenneth and Patricia approved of him? Hadn't they expected her and Tom to last?

She remembered Patricia broaching the subject, wishing more for her best friend. Elizabeth had defended Tom then—saying how handsome and smart he was, how much she admired him.

And Patricia had sighed with pity.

Now Elizabeth understood why. She had wanted passion and love for her friend, not admiration.

"We weren't even decided on whether or not we wanted children," he said.

But she suspected he was decided. He didn't want them. While he hadn't told her as much over the past few months, she'd sensed his withdrawal.

"That's why you pulled away," she said. "I thought it was because I was emotional over Kenneth's and Patricia's deaths, and you're not comfortable with emotion."

"I'm not," he admitted. "Neither are you. That's why we're so compatible. That's why we've had such a great relationship, Elizabeth."

She nodded in agreement. "We were comfortable," she agreed. "We talked about work over dinner in exclusive restaurants. We attended plays and art gallery openings."

He smiled. "We loved that life."

"That's not my life anymore," she said.

And she realized that wasn't the life she wanted now. Maybe that had never been the life she'd really wanted—it was only what she'd thought she wanted. It had been her idea of success, the kind of life her parents had lived, still lived. Like Tom, they hadn't offered to help her with little Lizzie. They hadn't comforted and consoled her over the loss of her best friends. If not for Kenneth and Patricia, she might have never known about true love—about true emotion.

"You could sign over custody to her uncle," Tom suggested. And she knew it wasn't the first time he had made that suggestion; he'd just been more subtle about it before.

Anger surged through her, and she wanted to slap him again. Instead, she stared down at her hand, admiring the diamond ring one last time before she pulled it from her finger and handed it back to him.

"What are you doing?" he asked.

"What I should have done months ago," she said. "Giving back your ring."

He wouldn't reach for it. Only shook his head. "Elizabeth, you're not yourself. You shouldn't be making decisions like this."

"I'm more myself than I've been," she said. "And I know now that I never should have accepted your ring. I care about you, but I don't love you like a wife should love her husband."

He gasped as if she'd hurt him. "Elizabeth!"

But she only smiled. "And you don't love me." She actually wondered how much he even really cared. "Not like a husband should love his wife."

"Elizabeth, you've been through so much that I think you should consider this some more before you make any rash decisions," he said.

She laughed. "Nobody's ever accused me of being rash." She had planned out her entire life— her education, her career, even her mate...

Tom Wilson had fit that role—before she'd met Dalton Reyes.

Maybe Tom knew her better than she thought, because he glanced up at the ceiling and nodded. "It's him—isn't it? That FBI agent..."

"What's him?" she asked.

"He's the reason you're giving me back this ring." And finally he reached for it, closing his fingers around the big diamond.

Dalton was definitely part of the reason but

not the entire reason. "We're the reason," she insisted. "We're not right for each other."

He shook his head. "We were perfect." But he looked at her now as if she wasn't—as if she was far from perfect.

Because she'd rejected him? Or because she had fallen for the FBI agent? Could he see that love in her—that love she'd never felt for him?

She would have apologized, but she wasn't sorry—not now. Not with the way he was acting. Her memories back now, she knew that she would have broken up with him earlier. But then she hadn't wanted to hurt him. Now she realized that she couldn't hurt him.

Dalton had, though. Tom kept rubbing his jaw even as he finally got to his feet and headed toward the door. "You're going to get hurt," he warned her.

Fear chilled her, and she asked, "Is that a threat?"

He tensed and stopped his advance toward the front door. "What?"

"Are you threatening me?" Was he the one who'd hired the hit on her?

"I'm warning you," he said. "I think you've fallen for the FBI agent out of gratitude to him for saving your life. But he was only doing his job, Elizabeth. He doesn't love you. And once this case is over, he'll move on to the next one. He'll leave you."

"He will," she agreed. She had already accepted that. But she would enjoy whatever time she had with Dalton—because she loved him. She loved him the way Kenneth and Patricia had loved each other...if only Dalton loved her back.

Tom hesitated at the door. "What we had was good, Elizabeth. We were comfortable. I'll keep the ring. You'll want to wear it again."

She shook her head at his stubbornness and his arrogance. Why had she never noticed it before? She wouldn't be going back to Tom Wilson. Ever. She wanted more out of life than comfortable.

She wanted passion. She wanted love. She wanted Dalton Reyes.

HE WANTED DALTON REYES. Dead.

The FBI agent had a damn hero complex. He had to keep riding in to rescue the damsel in distress. He understood now why Hoover had failed in the job he had hired him to do.

Dalton Reyes was the reason. The FBI agent had shot the ex-con. And he'd shot *him*.

He winced as he wrapped another bandage around his waist. The bullet had gone through his side without hitting anything vital. But he had probably needed surgery or at least stitches to close the wound. Instead, he had taped and bandaged it. And he hoped that nobody noticed it.

It hurt like hell, though. And he had to watch that the wound didn't get infected.

He wanted Elizabeth dead. Yet. Still. But he wanted Dalton Reyes dead even more.

Chapter Eighteen

The first thing he noticed when she stepped inside the nursery was that the ring was gone. Nothing sparkled on her hand—nothing taunted him that she belonged to someone else.

But it didn't matter that the ring was gone. She didn't belong to him, either.

"He left?"

She nodded.

"Did he ask for his ring back?" he asked, although he doubted it.

Tom Wilson hadn't looked like an idiot. But then the man had been so stupid that he hadn't even realized she was missing. Or maybe he had hoped that she was missing.

Forever.

"I gave it back to him," she said.

"Why?" he asked. And he held his breath as he waited for her admission. Was it because of him? Because she had feelings for him, too?

"He suggested that I sign over custody of Lizzie to her uncle."

He tightened his arm around the little girl. "I should have hit him harder."

Her lips curved into a slight smile. "If it makes you feel better, I slapped him—right on his swollen jaw."

It made him feel better. And it made him feel more—love for her. "You yelled at me for hitting him."

"I didn't yell at you," she protested. "I thought it was unnecessary."

His hand that wasn't holding the child fisted. "It was very necessary. He was all over you."

"He was trying to make me remember him."

"Did it work?"

"I remember him," she replied. "I remember that I intended to give that ring back months ago, but I hadn't wanted to hurt him."

"You don't care so much now?" he asked. Hopefully. If she hadn't wanted to hurt him, she must have had feelings for him at some point. Hell, she'd accepted his ring, so she must have loved him once.

"I don't care at all now," she said. And her gaze met his, as if she was trying to tell him something. That she cared about someone else instead.

Or was he only wistfully imagining that?

"That's good," he said. And he returned her stare. But he could only give her a look.

He couldn't give her anything else—not until he'd kept all of the promises he had made to her. To find out who she was. To keep her safe. To find out who was trying to kill her. And now he had promised to find out the truth about her friends' deaths.

He couldn't make any more promises until he'd kept those. And if he couldn't keep those…

"How was Trooper Littlefield?" she asked.

He closed his eyes to break their connection. He couldn't look at her and keep from her the information the trooper had given him. That it might have been Patricia—her best friend since they were kids—who had been the killer…

She wouldn't be able to handle that; she was already devastated from having to relive their loss as if it had just happened all over again.

"Is he going to be okay?" she asked.

"Yes," he assured her. "He will recover from the head injury."

"And he's had no loss of memory?" she asked.

"No." In fact, he had remembered everything very well.

She sighed. "He still doesn't believe me that someone else…" She trailed off, as if not wanting to discuss the baby's parents' deaths in front of little Lizzie.

He laid the sleeping child back down in her crib. Maybe she would stay there tonight—as long as no one else broke into her home. Dalton would make damn sure no one else broke into her home.

He followed Elizabeth out into the hall, but she didn't stop there—she continued to the master bedroom. And she held open the door for him and closed it once he stepped inside with her. His gaze went automatically to the bed, where they had made love the night before. The sheets were still tangled. She hadn't made it.

Her gaze followed his, and her face flushed with embarrassment. "I didn't have time to make the bed. After what happened last night, I didn't want Marta to come back here. Not until we know it's safe."

"There are guards outside," he said. "As long as you don't authorize them to let someone come up to the house, you'll be safe."

"But the man last night…" She shuddered.

Was still out there.

He pulled her into his arms, offering comfort for her fears.

She linked her arms around his neck and clung to him. "I'm overreacting," she said. "He's dead now."

"No, he's not," he corrected her.

She eased away from him and peered up into his face. "But you showed me his picture…"

"That man is dead," he said. "The ex-con is dead. But he was already dead when someone broke into the house. Someone else broke in here last night."

She tensed in his arms. "Someone else broke in."

"We suspected that there was someone else," he reminded her. "Someone that hired the ex-con."

"Someone I know," she murmured. "Someone I trust." She trembled in his arms as her fears returned.

He pulled her closer, enfolding her in his embrace. "That's why you can't let anyone in here," he said. "You were right to tell Marta to stay away."

"Marta would never hurt anyone," she protested. And she tried to pull back, but he held her tightly.

"You can't trust anyone," he said.

"What about you?" she asked. "Can I trust you?"

"I'm the only one you can trust," he said. "I would never hurt you."

Her lips curved into a slight, sad smile. "Don't lie to me."

"Elizabeth…" But before he could say anything

else, she rose on tiptoe and pressed her lips to his. He hadn't intended to make love to her tonight. He hadn't wanted to risk being distracted in case someone tried to break in again.

But there were guards blocking the driveway and watching the house. Nobody would get past them without him at least being forewarned. Even if the guards weren't there, he wasn't sure that he would have been able to resist her.

She undressed him—as he had undressed before for her. She removed his holster and gun and put them on the table beside the bed. Then she slowly, teasingly, undid the buttons on his shirt. Her fingertips skimmed over the muscles of his chest, teasing him as her hand traveled down to his belt.

He resisted the urge to take over—to hurry. He understood that she needed to be in control. She was a strong woman whose life was currently beyond her control. So he let her drive him crazy.

She made love to him with her mouth and her body. And finally she collapsed on his chest. Tears trailed from her face onto his neck as she snuggled into him.

He wasn't sure why she was crying. Because of her friends. Because she was in danger. She had so many reasons. So he just stroked her back until her cries subsided and she finally slept. He couldn't sleep, though—not even knowing there were guards outside. He had to stay vigilant.

His phone, which sat next to the holstered gun, vibrated against the table. He grabbed it quickly—dreading that this would be a warning from those guards.

But he didn't recognize the number calling him. "Hello?"

"Agent Reyes?"

Keeping his voice low so he didn't awaken Elizabeth, he asked, "Yes, who is this?"

"I—I got your number from a state trooper," the raspy voice replied. "I—I have some information you need."

"What information is that?"

"I—I think I know where a guy is—a guy that you might have shot…"

He tensed. And Elizabeth murmured. He carefully rolled her over to the other side of the bed. Then he hurried out into the hall. "Where?"

"I think he's here at Pinebrook Stables," the voice replied in a raspy whisper. "The vet treated him for a wound that looked an awful lot like a gunshot wound."

It was the guy—from last night. "What's the address for the stables?" Dalton asked. "And how badly is he hurt?"

"Bad," the raspy voice replied.

Then it hadn't been Tom Wilson with whom

he'd tangled in the dining room the night before. The extent of that man's injuries was the swollen jaw Dalton had just given him. He hadn't had a gunshot wound, or he wouldn't have been able to manhandle Elizabeth the way he had.

"The vet wanted to call an ambulance," the informant continued, "but no matter how much pain the guy is in, he refused. He's gotta be in trouble…"

He would be once Dalton got ahold of him. He couldn't wait to end this, to keep another of his promises to Elizabeth—so that he would be able to make more.

ELIZABETH AWAKENED TO an empty bed again. But the house was quiet. No crashing sounds. No gunshots. But the eerie silence was just as unsettling. She pulled on her robe and stepped into the hall.

A faint cry drifted from the nursery, so she hurried into little Lizzie's room. A shadow stood over her crib. It could have been Dalton. But the child sounded distressed.

So she flipped on the lights and gasped as she realized the dark-haired man wasn't Dalton. He wasn't as muscular or as tall, and his eyes weren't as dark. Agent Jared Bell held the little girl—but he held her awkwardly and as far away from his body as his arms would reach, as if she might detonate if she got too close.

She reached for her daughter and caught her close. "What are you doing here?" she asked.

"Agent Reyes asked me to take over," he said.

Her heart shifted in her chest, pain squeezing it. What had happened? Had she scared him off?

"Why would he ask you to take over the case?" she asked. "He doesn't believe it's that serial killer who's after me."

"No, he doesn't," Agent Bell agreed. "And neither do I anymore. He only asked me to take over protection duty for the rest of the night."

"Protection duty," she said as she soothed the disgruntled child. "Not babysitting. You didn't have to try to pick her up." It was a miracle he hadn't dropped her with the way he'd been holding her.

"That was a mistake," he admitted with a shudder of unease as she changed the child's diaper. "I didn't think it would be that hard—not when Blaine Campbell, and even Reyes, make it look easy."

Dalton was good with little Lizzie. And with Elizabeth, too.

"Some people are probably naturals," she said. "I wasn't one. It took time and practice for me to get used to being around a little one." But, even before her death, Patricia had made certain to train her, as if she knew that someday Elizabeth would be taking over her mothering duties.

"I don't need any practice," Agent Bell said. "It's not like I ever intend to have kids."

"You don't?"

He shook his head. "Working for the Bureau is all-consuming. I don't have time for relationships, let alone a family."

She already knew Dalton felt the same way, but her heart grew heavy with disappointment. "But Agent Campbell has both. And Agent Stryker just got married."

He shrugged. "They're at different points in their careers than Reyes and I are," he said. "They can step back and do more training than fieldwork. We can't."

And she suspected that wasn't just because of where they were in their careers but because of their personalities. They lived for fieldwork. They were fearless. But being fearless tended to get people killed—because they didn't recognize and respect the danger.

"Where did Dalton go?" she asked with a terrifying sense of foreboding that he had put himself in danger again.

"He's following a lead," Agent Bell replied.

She dimly remembered his phone vibrating on the bedside table and then the deep rumble of his voice. "He got a call earlier."

He nodded. "That was the lead."

"He didn't go off alone, did he?" she asked.

"He didn't want any backup," Agent Bell admitted. "He didn't think he needed it."

Her pulse quickened with fear for his life. "He thinks he's invincible."

"From everything I've heard about him and witnessed myself," Agent Bell said, "I kind of think he is, too."

She wasn't convinced—not after everything she'd recently gone through. Even the person hired to kill her had died. Nobody was invincible. "You should have gone with him."

"He wanted me here—to protect you," he said. "That was more important to him."

Her heart warmed with hope that he seemed to care about her—really care about her—as more than just a case. But her fear for him overwhelmed that hope. "Than his own safety?"

Jared Bell shrugged. "I wouldn't worry about him." He obviously wasn't. "He survived the street gang he grew up in and then turned on—"

"Because of his grandmother," she said defensively, in case Agent Bell thought Dalton had betrayed his gang members. They had betrayed him first. "He turned on them because they killed her—the woman who'd raised him."

Jared's caramel-colored eyes widened in surprise and he sucked in a sharp breath. "I didn't know that."

She suspected it was a story that Dalton had

told few people. Why had he told her? Why was he letting her so deeply into his life if he didn't intend to stay around once he apprehended whoever was trying to kill her?

But he wouldn't be able to share her life if he lost his while trying to apprehend that killer. He shouldn't have gone off alone.

HE WAITED IN the dark, following the beacon of the SUV's headlamp beams traveling up the circular driveway to the deserted horse ranch. There was only one vehicle coming up that road. And, using the night-vision scope on his rifle, he could spy only one shadow inside the vehicle, behind the steering wheel.

A smile spread across his face. This had been easier than he had even anticipated it could be. He waited until the SUV got a little closer—until that shadow behind the wheel was directly in his scope—then he squeezed the trigger.

Chapter Nineteen

Elizabeth couldn't get back to sleep. Maybe it was because she missed the warmth and comfort of Dalton's strong arms holding her and the reassuring rise and fall of his muscular chest beneath her cheek. Or maybe she couldn't sleep because that terrifying sense of foreboding continued to grip her.

Hours must have passed since he had gotten that call. But he wasn't back. And she worried that he wouldn't be able to come back.

Jared Bell had faith in him. And so did she. But whoever was trying to kill her was determined to finish the job, and like her, he must have realized that Dalton wouldn't let that happen.

While he was alive.

He wouldn't break that promise he'd made her. While he was alive.

But if he were dead…

No. She wouldn't consider that possibility. She would believe—as he and Agent Bell believed—

that he was invincible. Nothing could happen to Dalton.

She hadn't even told him she loved him. She should have told him. She had tried showing him tonight—when she'd made love to him with all her heart and soul. She hoped he had understood that hadn't been gratitude. She felt so much more than gratitude for him.

While she wasn't sleeping, she lay alone in the tangled sheets of the bed she'd shared with Dalton such a short time ago. If she stepped outside the door, she would have to talk to Jared—have to listen to his empty assurances. He didn't make promises the way Dalton did.

But while she lay in the dark, she heard that strange sound again—that vibration of the silent ring of a cell phone. And she realized it was coming through the baby monitor. Jared must have gone back into the nursery. For a man so uncomfortable and awkward with children, he was strangely drawn to little Lizzie. But then, the precious girl was as magnetic and magical as her mother had been.

Elizabeth had already lost her best friends. She couldn't lose the love of her life, too.

"Agent Bell." The words came clearly through the monitor as Jared answered his call.

She couldn't hear his caller, though. So she had to wait, with an unbearable pressure on her chest, while Agent Bell listened. His response was a heartfelt curse.

And her heart plummeted.

"How badly is he hurt?" he asked.

"No!" The protest burst from her lips even though she knew the injured man was Dalton. She'd known that he wasn't invincible. She jumped out of bed and hurried down the hall to the nursery.

Jared opened the door and stepped into the hall to join her. But his cell phone was still pressed to his ear as he listened to whoever had called him.

It wasn't Dalton. Because he'd asked how badly *he* was hurt. And she knew *he* was Dalton.

"What happened?" she asked—too anxious to wait until his call was done. "How is he?"

Not dead. He couldn't be dead.

Jared shook his head, and her heart stopped beating for one beat before resuming at a frantic pace, hammering away in her chest.

"No!"

"I'll check back soon," he said into the phone before quickly clicking it off. Then he reached for her.

She hadn't even realized that her legs were shaking so badly that they had nearly buckled beneath her. But she couldn't feel—not even his hands on her shoulders holding her up—since fear paralyzed her.

"Is he dead?" she asked. "Is Dalton dead?"

Jared shook his head again. "No, he's not."

"But he's hurt," she said. "I heard you over the baby monitor. He's hurt."

"He was shot," Jared replied.

She felt a sharp jab to her heart and sucked in a breath of pain. "Oh, no! How bad is it?"

"I don't know yet," he admitted. "He's en route to the hospital right now."

"We need to go," she said. "We need to meet him there." She had to see him—had to see how badly he was wounded. She had to hold his hand, the way he had held hers when she'd been hurt.

But Agent Bell shook his head again. "No, it's too dangerous."

"How?"

"We could be driven off the road or attacked as we leave the house," he pointed out. "We can't leave here."

"You may not care about your fellow agent," she accused him, "but I do." She didn't just care; she loved him. So much. "I want to be there for him."

"I will be there for him," he said. "By keeping you here. Your safety is his priority and my responsibility now. I won't let him down by putting you in danger."

Panic was making it hard for her to draw a deep breath into her lungs. She had to be with

Dalton. "You don't know that we'll be in danger if we go to the hospital."

He gestured toward the closed door of the nursery. "It won't be just your life you're risking," he pointed out, "if we put her in the car with us and it gets run off the road."

"You don't know that'll happen," she insisted.

"I'm a profiler," he reminded her. "I'm not Dalton Reyes. I don't drive like he does."

"Then have someone else bring me to the hospital," she suggested. "One of the troopers outside. And you can stay with Lizzie." She cared more about the child than herself; she'd rather have him keeping Lizzie safe.

Panic flashed across his face now, leaving it stark. "No. Absolutely not."

"But—"

"Keeping you safe is my responsibility," he reiterated. "We're staying here."

"What makes you think we're safe here?" she asked. "Don't you think that Dalton was shot to get him out of the way? And now that he's out of the way, that person is going to try to get to me again. It doesn't matter if we're at the hospital or if we're here."

"There are guards outside the house," he said. "And I'm inside with you. You're safe here."

She shivered as that foreboding rushed over her again. And she shook her head. "No. I won't be safe anywhere." Especially not now with Dalton wounded.

How badly was he hurt?

Would he make it back to her?

Ever?

HE WAS GLAD THAT, when he'd cleared out Hoover's motel room, he had saved the uniform the ex-con had taken off Trooper Littlefield. Without it, he wouldn't have made it past the deputy blocking the end of the driveway. The poor man had had no idea what had hit him...

Just like whoever was guarding Elizabeth would have no idea what had hit him, either. Leaving the squad car blocking the end of the driveway, he headed up toward the house.

The radio he'd taken off the deputy squawked. "This is Agent Bell," the caller announced. "Is everything clear outside?"

He hesitated answering but finally pressed the button. "I've noticed a light shining in the trees at the back of the house. It could be someone walking around with a flashlight. Should I go check it out?"

"Yes," the agent replied. "But be careful. I'm pretty sure the suspect is going to make his move tonight."

He was right. The suspect was making his move right now...onto the front porch. But the beauty was that nobody suspected *him*. He would get away with murder.

Again.

A shadow darkened the glass of the front door. Had Agent Bell heard him step onto the porch? He moved quickly, backing against the side of the house so that he wouldn't be seen.

Yet.

But the front door creaked open.

God, he was making this easy for him.

Agent Bell stepped out, gun drawn.

He waited in those shadows—just waited, his breath held, until the man stepped close enough. Then he struck, lashing out with the butt of the gun he'd taken off the deputy. Just like the deputy, Agent Bell never saw him.

He dropped to the porch with a heavy thud. He was either unconscious or dead. It didn't matter which. He wouldn't regain consciousness in time to save Elizabeth.

No one could save her now.

The front door creaked again. "Agent Bell?" a female voice called out. "Are you out here?"

The agent didn't even groan. He couldn't hear her.

"Jared?" she called out with obvious apprehension now. "Jared, where are you?"

Maybe she would step out, too, and make it all

so easy for him. But instead, she pulled the door shut. The lock clicked as she turned the dead bolt.

Still in the shadows, he grinned. It didn't matter that she'd locked the door. He had a key. He would get to her. She was as good as already dead.

PAIN RADIATED THROUGHOUT Dalton's chest. It wasn't just the bullet. The vest had taken most of the impact of that. And it had only grazed his arm before hitting the vest. His pain was actually panic—the panic that he had left Elizabeth and the little girl in danger.

"Get the doctor in here," he told Blaine Campbell. "I need to get out of here."

"You need stitches in that arm," Blaine said.

Dalton glanced down at the blood-soaked bandage. "It's fine."

"You lost a lot of blood."

He shrugged. "Not like you did."

Blaine had taken a bullet in the neck months before and was lucky to be alive. But then, Blaine Campbell was a lucky man. Dalton had a horrible feeling that his luck was running out.

"This is nothing." He swung his legs over the gurney and stood up, but his legs weren't quite as steady as he'd counted on and he stumbled forward.

Blaine caught one of his arms while another

man grabbed his other. "Hey," Trooper Littlefield said. "You need to wait for the doctor."

"I'm fine," he said. "It's Elizabeth I'm worried about."

"Jared Bell is with Elizabeth," Blaine reminded him. Blaine had been with him—crouched down in the backseat. He had insisted on coming along even though Dalton had thought he could handle the situation alone.

He cursed himself. "I knew it was an ambush..." But he'd still walked right into it. "And the only reason someone would want to take me out is to get to Elizabeth."

"From what I understand, a lot of people would like to take you out," Blaine reminded him.

"In Chicago," he agreed. "Not here. I barely know anybody here."

"Somebody could have followed you," Blaine pointed out. He had been followed—on that case that had nearly claimed his life.

It wasn't just pride that had him shaking his head. He was certain. "This isn't about me. It's about Elizabeth."

Trooper Littlefield uttered a regretful and agitated sigh. "Maybe it's about her friends," he said. "The more I think about that crime scene..."

"You think she's right? It was no murder-suicide?" Blaine asked.

Dalton had already determined as much.

"The gun was in Kenneth Cunningham's hand," Littlefield said. "But he died first. He couldn't have killed her after he died."

"Someone staged the scene," Blaine agreed. "Why? And what does that have to do with Elizabeth?"

"Whoever did it wants to shut her up," Dalton said. "She won't stop fighting for justice for her friends and for their daughter."

"She won't stop," Trooper Littlefield agreed. "She was adamant that her friends were so in love that they would have never hurt each other."

Dalton nodded. "She really believes that."

"She's biased," Blaine pointed out.

"She's not the only one," Trooper Littlefield said. "Pretty much everyone that knew the Cunninghams or had ever met them agrees with her."

Pretty much everyone…

The doctor stepped into the room. "What are you doing out of bed?" he asked Dalton.

"I have to leave," he replied. He had to get the hell out of there. Now.

"You have to get stitches," the doctor said—just as Blaine had moments before.

"I have to get back to Elizabeth," he insisted—because he had figured it out.

"Jared is with Elizabeth," Blaine reiterated. "He'll keep her safe. You don't need to worry."

But he was worried. Because someone had

tried to take him out for a reason, and he believed that reason was to get to Elizabeth.

He held up a hand—holding the doctor and his suture kit back. "Let me call him."

Blaine cursed as he fumbled his cell phone out of his jeans pocket. "I promised I'd call him back, but I haven't yet."

Dalton held out his hand for Blaine's cell, which the other agent handed over with a sigh. He pushed the redial button. The phone rang once, twice, three times and then four and five before going to voice mail.

"Special Agent Jared Bell. I am currently unavailable, but leave me your name and number, and I will return your call."

"What the hell's going on?" Dalton shouted into the phone, but also at his friends. "If he's waiting for your call, why did it go to voice mail?"

But he knew. And from their faces, so did they. Something had happened to Jared that had, at the least, incapacitated him. And now Elizabeth was alone and unprotected. He headed for the door, and this time nobody tried to stop him. Instead, they hurried along with him.

No matter how fast he drove, he probably wouldn't get to her in time. He had broken one of his promises to Elizabeth. He hadn't protected her.

Chapter Twenty

Fear gripped Elizabeth. Fear for Dalton. How badly was he hurt? Would he survive his gunshot wound?

She also felt fear for Agent Jared Bell. Where had he gone? He had just disappeared. But she knew better than to risk going outside to search for him. She had no gun. No weapon that would defend her and little Lizzie from a gun or a killer.

Somewhere she had a business card for Special Agent Blaine Campbell. She could call him for help. If only she could find his card...

She fumbled around in the drawers of the desk in the office on the first floor. The white-paneled room was next to the dining room—where Dalton had struggled so recently with the intruder.

Where *was* Jared Bell? She had heard no sounds of a struggle. She'd only heard the creak of the front door opening and closing. And footsteps on the porch.

Wood creaked and groaned as someone stepped

onto the porch again. Her pulse quickened with fear. But maybe it was just Jared returning. Maybe he'd gone down the driveway to talk to the guards by the road—to warn them that someone could be coming for her.

Not could be. Was.

She knew it. That was why Dalton had been shot. Because of her.

Guilt joined her fear. If only Dalton hadn't been so intent on keeping the promises he'd made to her. If only he hadn't been so good at protecting her...

Then maybe someone wouldn't have been so intent on getting him out of the way. She had to get to the hospital. If that was Jared Bell on the porch, she would convince him to take her to Dalton. She had to tell him she loved him.

More boards creaked as the person crossed the porch. Then the doorbell pealed. And she remembered locking the door. She had locked out the agent. Her breath shuddered out with relief, and she rushed to the door. But when she pulled it open, it wasn't Agent Bell standing on the front porch.

Tom Wilson stood in front of her, his face flushed, his hair mussed. Alcohol emanated from him as if he'd soaked himself in it.

"Eliz...a...beth..." He sounded as if he was

trying to sing but was just slurring. Tom Wilson didn't sing—not even in the shower.

"What are you doing here?"

She thought he had left town and returned to Chicago after she'd given him back his ring. But apparently he had gone to a bar instead and had been there ever since. She could never remember him having more than a glass of wine with dinner and champagne on New Year's. When had he started drinking?

He stumbled across the threshold into the foyer. "I have to talk to you, Elizabeth."

She couldn't deal with Tom right now—not when she was so worried about Dalton. And about Agent Bell.

"We have nothing more to say to each other," she insisted. They had been over a long time ago; she shouldn't have been wearing his ring anymore. She actually never should have accepted it.

"That's not true, Elizabeth."

They were done—whether or not his pride could accept it.

"You'll want to hear what I have to tell you," he insisted with an aggression she had never seen in him before. And suddenly his words weren't so slurred.

Had he faked the drunkenness so that she would think him harmless and let him inside the house? But how had he gotten past the guards at the end of the driveway? She was certain that Dalton had given orders that Tom Wilson never be allowed up to the house again.

"How did you get up here?" she asked.

"I walked."

"Nobody stopped you at the street?"

He shook his head. "Nobody was there—just a police car blocked the end of the driveway."

"There was no trooper or agent by the car?" she asked. And if not, where had he gone? Had he disappeared with Agent Bell?

"No." He glanced around the room, as if checking now to see if she was alone. "Isn't *he* here?"

"Who?" But she knew who he was referring to and it wasn't Agent Bell.

"That FBI agent you're in love with," he said. "He's gone already." And a smug smile crossed a face she'd once considered so handsome.

Fear chilled her, lifting goose bumps on her skin. And she asked, "What did you do to him?"

"Me?" he asked, his blue eyes widening in shock. "You think I did something to him?"

"He was shot."

His brow furrowed with confusion. "Have you ever known me to shoot a gun?"

She shook her head. But she wasn't sure that she had ever really known him at all. She already knew Dalton Reyes so much better than she'd ever known the man to whom she'd been engaged for two years.

"I haven't," she said. "But that doesn't mean you don't know how to shoot—that you don't own a gun."

He furrowed his brow, as if trying to figure out what she was saying. But she didn't believe that he was actually drunk anymore.

"We've dated for years," she said. "But we never actually spent that much time together. We never lived together. I don't know what you own. I don't know what you know."

"Are you sure that your memory is back?" he asked. "Because you're not making any sense. But then, you've not been making much sense since Kenneth and Patricia died."

She cocked her head, trying to understand what he meant. "Because I'm determined to keep my promise to them and raise little Lizzie?" she asked. Like Dalton Reyes, she kept the promises she made—or she would as long as she was alive. "I'm not giving her up."

"You would rather give me up instead?" And he was all wounded male pride again. "It's that easy for you to just give me back my ring and walk away from all the years we've known each other."

"We don't know each other at all," she said, "if you expect me to give up my goddaughter."

"It's not just her you're being unreasonable about," he said. "You're being unreasonable about their deaths. Why can't you just accept that it was a murder-suicide? Why do you have to keep going to authorities—keep pushing them to reopen the investigation?"

She shivered now as fear chilled her. "Why do you care?" she asked.

"Because you're making a fool of yourself."

"Is that the real reason?" she wondered. "Or is there another reason you don't want the investigation into their deaths reopened?"

His flushed face drained of all color. "What the hell reason could I have?"

"Because you were involved," she suggested. "Because you wanted Patricia for yourself."

He laughed. "I didn't even like Patricia."

That surprised her more than anything else. Everyone who had met her had loved Patricia; she had been that special. Elizabeth was certain that she and Dalton would have become fast friends. "Why not?"

"Because she didn't like me," he said. "Because she didn't think I was good enough for her best friend. I didn't want Patricia in my life at all. And I didn't want her in yours."

"Is that why you did it?" she asked. "Is that why you killed them?"

"You're crazy!" he said as color rushed back into his face.

She was crazy to have let him inside the house. And she was crazy with fear.

"Is that why you want to kill me?" she asked. "Because I keep pushing to have that investigation reopened?"

He lurched forward, reaching for her. Before she could turn and run, he caught her. His hands gripping her shoulders, he shook her.

She needed to fight him. But that shaking left her head reeling with dizziness and nausea. Her memory had returned, but she wasn't completely recovered from the concussion. Summoning her strength, she wriggled and twisted, trying to break free of his hold. And then suddenly his hands slipped away as he dropped to the floor in front of her.

She looked up—expecting to see Agent Bell or even Dalton standing where Tom had stood. But it was Kenneth's brother, Gregory Cunningham, wielding a gun. He must have struck Tom with the butt of it.

"Oh, my God," she said with a shaky breath of relief. "I thought he was going to kill me. Thank you…"

But her gratitude turned to nerves as he stared at her with a strange expression, with no expression on a face that had always reminded her so much of Kenneth's—until now. Now he looked nothing like his brother in appearance or demeanor. And, for some reason, he wore an ill-fitting uniform. A trooper's uniform. From the badge on the pocket, she realized it was Trooper Littlefield's uniform. Gregory turned the barrel of the gun toward her.

"What—what are you doing?" she asked.

A phone vibrated. He reached into his pocket for it, but his grip didn't loosen on the gun. "Agent Campbell keeps calling…"

"That's Agent Bell's phone," she realized. "What did you do to him?"

He shrugged. "I'm not sure if he's dead or just extremely unconscious."

She cursed him.

"Agent Campbell must be calling to report to him about Reyes's condition," he mused. "Now *him*—I'm sure *he's* dead."

She gasped as pain stabbed her heart. "No…"

"I had to get him out of the way," he explained. "He kept messing up my plans for you."

"Why?" she asked. "Why do you want to kill me?"

"I don't *want* to," he assured her. "I've always liked you, Elizabeth. I've always admired your drive and spunk. I even admire your loyalty."

She edged backward—toward that office. If she could get inside and lock the doors…

"Then why have you been trying to kill me?" she asked. He was really the crazy one. Had he always been? Was that why Patricia and Kenneth had left her their daughter instead of him? She had always wondered.

"It's really Kenneth's fault," Gregory said. "I thought my brother would leave me custody of Lizzie."

She gasped again, with another jab of pain. "You killed them."

"That was Kenneth's fault, too," he said. "He cut me off. Stopped giving me money. And without money, I'd lose Miranda."

She flinched because she had advised Kenneth to stop giving his brother money that he'd lost anyway. Gregory had used Kenneth's loans for risky investments—in get-rich-quick schemes to finance his wife's lavish lifestyle. If he didn't keep buying her the expensive clothes and cars she craved, his wife had threatened to leave him.

Elizabeth remembered Patricia's disgust that her sister-in-law cared more about the money than she had about her husband. Patricia had believed in her vows—in sickness and health, in until death do we part...

Tears stung Elizabeth's eyes as she realized that death had parted her friends. No. She had to believe they were still together—that they would always be together. If Gregory killed her, as he had Dalton, would she reunite with him?

But she wasn't about to give up her life without a fight. She slid a little closer to the doors of the den that she had left open. "So you killed them because you thought you would get their money," she continued. "You don't care about Lizzie."

"I'll take care of her," he promised.

She didn't trust his promises the way she had Dalton's. She wouldn't put it past him to get rid of the little girl, too—once he was awarded custody.

"Kenneth and Patricia wanted me to take care of her," she said. She'd assumed it was because they hadn't liked Gregory's mercenary wife. Now she realized that they might have known there was something wrong with him—that his desperation had driven him to madness.

"Kenneth and Patricia always got everything they wanted," he said. "The degrees. The jobs. The house. The kid. Their lives were perfect."

And he had obviously envied them that perfection.

He glanced down at where Tom lay unconscious on the floor, and she edged into the doorway of the den. "I should thank Wilson for showing up like he did," Gregory said. "He's making this easy for me."

"You're going to do to us what you did with Kenneth and Patricia," she said, feeling nausea all over again at his sick plan. "You're going to make it look like a murder-suicide."

"It worked the first time," he said.

She shook her head. "Dalton reopened the investigation."

He shrugged. "Reyes is gone."

"Agent Bell—"

"Gone, too," he said.

She shuddered at his callousness. "Agent Campbell will look into everything, then," she said. The men were too close to not look out for each other—even if some of them were gone.

"And he'll blame Tom Wilson for it all," Gregory assured her. And as he glanced down at the man again, she stepped back and slammed the office doors between them. She twirled the dead bolts even though she doubted they would keep him out very long.

Already he pounded on the doors. And as he pounded, a cry rang out from above as the noise woke little Lizzie.

She crossed the den to the exterior wall and pulled up a window. The opening was big. She could climb out onto the porch and disappear into the darkness of the acreage surrounding the house.

But then the pounding stopped.

"I'll go get her," Gregory shouted through the locked doors.

Elizabeth froze with fear—just inches from saving herself. She couldn't do it. She stepped away from the open window and walked back to the door.

His shaky sigh emanated through the doors before he added, "I probably should have killed her with them—then I would have inherited the money straightaway. I wouldn't have had to go after you. It would have been simpler."

"But you care about her," she reminded him. "She's an innocent child."

"She loved her parents, Elizabeth," he said. "Isn't it kinder to reunite her with them?"

She quickly twisted the dead bolts and pulled open the doors. "No," she said. "Please don't hurt her."

She had promised Kenneth and Patricia that she would take care of Lizzie as if she was her own. She would gladly die for the child.

"YOU'RE GOING TO bleed to death," Blaine warned him with a curse.

Blood saturated Dalton's sleeve. But it was only a trickle from the wound now. He didn't care about that, though.

"And you shouldn't be driving," Blaine added, gripping the armrest and the dash as Dalton careened around a curve.

He hadn't trusted anyone else to drive as fast

as he could—as he had to in order to get to Elizabeth and the little girl. But no matter how fast he drove, he worried he wouldn't get to them in time.

"Bell won't answer his phone," Trooper Littlefield said from the backseat. He'd taken Campbell's cell and had kept hitting the redial.

"He would answer," Dalton said, "if he could." He had gotten to know the man well over the past few days. He was every bit as focused an agent as Dalton usually was.

Bell was already gone. Elizabeth probably was, too.

The next curve brought the house into view— lights burned in several of the windows. He nearly struck a rental car parked near the police car at the end of the driveway.

"Nobody's here," Blaine said as he took in the empty police car. "I can get out and see if the keys are inside and move it."

But before he could reach for the door handle, Dalton backed up and slammed his SUV into the patrol car—pushing it out of his way. Then he pressed hard on the accelerator and tore up the driveway. As he slammed it into Park and jumped out, he heard the gunshot.

Just as he'd worried, he was too late.

Chapter Twenty-One

A scream of pain tore from Elizabeth's throat. Loss wrenched her heart as Tom's blood spattered her face. He dropped to the floor as he had earlier. But this time she doubted he was just unconscious.

He was dead. While she didn't love him anymore, she once had, so she still cared what happened to him. She cared that he had been killed—because of her. Just like so many others had lost their lives because of her.

Dalton. Her chest hurt, panic and pain pressing so hard on her heart that she couldn't draw a breath. Dalton was already dead. Now Tom.

And she was going to be next.

At least she hoped she was going to be next. Gregory kept glancing up—where the little girl could be heard screaming, too. The terror in her voice broke Elizabeth's heart. She ached to hold her, to soothe her fears and dry all those tears—to take care of her as she had promised Kenneth and Patricia she would.

Gregory Cunningham moved, as if heading toward the stairs. She almost reached out to stop him, but Tom's body lay between them and she nearly fell over him—nearly fell on top of him.

"Please don't hurt Lizzie," she pleaded with the madman—hoping to appeal to his sense of decency, even though she doubted that he had one after all the pain he had already caused.

"She's an innocent child," Elizabeth continued. "She's your niece." But Kenneth had been his brother and that hadn't stopped him from killing him. "She's the only part left of Kenneth and Patricia—the best part." That was what they had always said. "The best part of the best people..."

He turned back to her, and tears glistened in his eyes. Maybe he had a conscience, after all. "I didn't want to do it, you know." But his tears cleared as he justified the horror he'd done. "But Kenny gave me no choice. He stopped giving me money."

That was her fault. She had advised Kenneth that it was time to cut off his brother. Her friends had died because of her. Now Dalton and probably Jared Bell and Tom next.

"Promise me you won't hurt her," she pleaded with him again. "I don't care about *me*. Just please take care of Lizzie. Raise her the way that Kenneth and Patricia wanted her to be raised."

His face—so like his brother's—twisted into a grimace of pain and regret. "Elizabeth..."

"They wanted her to always feel loved," she said, glancing up at the ceiling from which the little girl's cries seemed to emanate. "To be confident and self-assured and fearless."

Like Dalton. He was confident and self-assured and fearless, but he'd wound up dead because of that. Because of her.

Tears streamed from Gregory's eyes. "I'm really sorry about this, Elizabeth."

"Just promise me..." But she knew that even if he gave it, it wouldn't be like the heartfelt promises Dalton Reyes had made her. Gregory's promise would be an empty one. He had already threatened to kill the child. Maybe that had been an empty threat—only meant to draw her out of the office so that he could kill her. "Don't hurt her."

"I won't," Gregory said. "I couldn't harm her before. I won't be able to do it now. I need the money—that's all, Elizabeth."

She could have tried to lie—tried to claim that the money was gone. But Kenneth and Patricia had been fanatical about earning and saving money, and they had already set up a trust fund for their daughter. Unlike his brother, Kenneth's investments had paid off well. There was money;

she just hadn't realized that someone would have killed them over it.

And now her.

She bit her lip so she wouldn't plead for her life. It was no use trying to appeal to Gregory Cunningham's sense of decency. If he had one, he wouldn't have already killed so many people. She had already accepted that she was to be the next—and hopefully the last.

So she closed her eyes and waited for the bullet.

DALTON HAD SLIPPED silently into the house— through an open window in the den. Before he'd found the open window, he had found Jared Bell lying on the porch, blood pooled beneath his head.

He had been certain that the man, whom he was just now beginning to consider a friend, was dead. But when he'd reached down for Jared's throat, he had felt a steadily beating pulse. Like Elizabeth, the blow hadn't killed the profiler. But he needed an ambulance.

Blaine had gestured that he would make the call for help. The other agent had kept pace with Dalton on his mad dash to the house. But they had hesitated to burst inside before they assessed the situation. So Dalton had slipped through that open window alone.

Blaine and Littlefield were waiting for his cue.

But he couldn't give it and risk one of them startling Gregory Cunningham into killing Elizabeth. He had realized it was him at the hospital when Littlefield had admitted that everyone had shared Elizabeth's opinion of Kenneth and Patricia Cunningham—that they were a loving couple who would have never harmed each other.

The only person who'd offered a different opinion had been the man who'd killed them and tried to make it look like a murder-suicide. Kenneth's own brother.

Now the man intended to kill Elizabeth and not just to keep her from reopening an investigation into the Cunninghams' deaths. Alone in the darkness of the den, Dalton had listened to their conversation through the doors that had been left open like the window.

Through those open doors, he had also seen Tom Wilson lying on the foyer floor. Like Jared Bell, blood had pooled beneath him. The shot he'd heard, as he'd stepped out of his SUV, must have been fired at Wilson.

It was too late to help him. But he could help Elizabeth. Maybe...

He had heard everything Gregory had said— his confession about the murder of his brother and sister-in-law. He had also heard everything Elizabeth had said—had heard her negotiating for the little girl's life. She was willing to give up her own life to keep the child safe. As safe as she would be with a killer for a guardian.

In Elizabeth, Kenneth and Patricia had chosen the right guardian for their daughter. They had chosen someone who loved little Lizzie every bit as much as they had.

Dalton didn't want to lose either one of them. The child had stopped crying. Either Blaine or Littlefield must have made it up to the nursery without Gregory noticing them. One of them was soothing her fears. At least she was safe now.

It was up to him to secure Elizabeth's safety. But if he shot Gregory Cunningham and the guy squeezed the trigger of his gun...

The barrel was pointed directly at Elizabeth's head. Gregory was doing it again—exactly as he had killed his brother and his sister-in-law. First he'd killed the man and then the woman.

Had Patricia done the same thing Elizabeth had—had she negotiated for her daughter's life and then closed her eyes to accept her gruesome fate?

For Elizabeth, Dalton would fight fate. He would keep his promise to her and make sure that she stayed safe. So he stepped out of the shadows of the den.

Gregory Cunningham caught sight of him. His eyes widened with shock, and his face paled. He must have been pretty certain that he had killed

Dalton back at the abandoned horse ranch—so certain that at first he'd probably thought he was seeing a ghost. But now, realizing that Dalton was real and alive, Gregory Cunningham swung the barrel of his gun toward him.

But Dalton was already squeezing the trigger of his gun.

If Gregory fired now, the bullet would hit him. Not Elizabeth. For Elizabeth, Dalton would gladly give up his life.

ELIZABETH FLINCHED AT the sound of the gunshot—so close to her head. She waited for the pain. But it never came. Instead, she felt more drops across her face. Blood...

This time it had to be hers. Didn't it?

But where was the pain? Or was she numb? Paralyzed?

Dead?

"Elizabeth..." Dalton's deep voice called to her.

From the beyond?

Then fingertips skimmed over her face. "Are you okay?" he asked. "Were you hit?"

She opened her eyes to his face—to his dark eyes staring at her with concern. And something else.

She must have died. Or at least she was unconscious and dreaming. Because that emotion couldn't really be in his eyes—although she was certain it was in hers.

"You're alive!" she exclaimed. "You're alive!" She threw her arms around his neck and clung to him. "I thought he shot you!"

"He did," Dalton replied matter-of-factly, as if his gunshot wound was of no consequence.

She pulled back and then she saw the blood, which soaked the sleeve of his dark green shirt. "You're still bleeding!" she exclaimed. The fabric was warm and damp. She jerked her hand away—afraid that she'd hurt him—and her palm was stained red with his blood. "Didn't they treat you at the hospital?"

"I couldn't stay," he said. "Not when I knew you were in danger. And Jared wasn't answering his cell."

She covered her mouth to hold back a cry of alarm and regret. Poor Agent Bell.

"He disappeared," she said. "I don't know what happened to him." But she suspected that it wasn't good.

"I found him on the porch. Blaine called an ambulance for him." But from the concern in his voice, he wasn't sure the ambulance would arrive in time to help his friend.

Sirens whined in the distance as emergency vehicles rushed to the scene. Fortunately, Gregory hadn't noticed those sirens, or he would have shot her before help could have arrived for her.

Before Dalton had arrived.

"You saved me." As he had so many times before. But he needed help now.

Hopefully, the ambulance would be able to get up the driveway. Tom had said that it was blocked.

Tom...

Her breath hitched with regret over all the lives that had been taken—because of greed. If only she hadn't told Kenneth to cut off Gregory.

Then they would all be alive. Her dearest friends would be able to raise their precious daughter. Little Lizzie had stopped crying. How was that possible with all the shooting? She had to be terrified from all the commotion.

Fear gripped her again. Dalton was here—with her. Who was with Lizzie?

Dalton had kept his promise to protect her. But had she failed in her promise to protect the little girl?

"Lizzie isn't crying," she pointed out. "She's been crying since Gregory shot Tom. Why would she stop now? Is there someone else in the house?"

"Yes," Dalton replied. "Blaine Campbell and Trooper Littlefield came with me from the hospital. One of them must be with her now."

She needed to be with her—to make sure that the little girl was really all right. But she couldn't leave Dalton—and not just because he was wounded. She couldn't leave Dalton because she loved him, and she was so grateful that he was alive. She had been so worried about him.

That fear must have been on her face yet, because Dalton assured her, "She's safe now. It's all over."

But just as her fears eased, she heard something else that had her tensing with fear. Someone groaned, and there was a flurry of movement on the floor.

She had thought that Dalton had killed Gregory—that it was his blood that had struck her face when she'd had eyes closed as she'd waited for death. But what if Dalton had only wounded the madman?

What if he was reaching for his gun again?

Dalton reached for his, drawing it from his holster. But would he be able to save her or himself?

Or would Gregory finish what he'd started so many months ago with Kenneth's and Patricia's murders?

Chapter Twenty-Two

"You're a fool," Ash Stryker called Dalton.

He glared at his happy friend. While Stryker and Claire had returned from their honeymoon, it was obviously far from over—if the guy's smiling face was anything to go by.

"Just a few short weeks ago you were begging me to be your best man," Dalton reminded him with just a slight exaggeration. "And now you're calling me a fool?"

"Because you are one," Blaine Campbell said from where he leaned against the brick wall of the living room of Dalton's condo.

They had invited themselves over to his place. He had thought to check up on him and make sure he was completely recovered from the gunshot wound—minimal though it had been. But now he felt as if they were staging some kind of intervention.

"Two against one?" he scoffed at their pitiful attempt to gang up on him. "These are my kind of odds, you know." Hell, he'd always taken on more than two at a time.

"They would have been," Blaine agreed. "If you'd had the guts to go for it."

Now they were talking over his head. "What do you mean?" Nobody had ever accused him of being a coward. A fool—well, that wasn't the first time.

"Elizabeth Schroeder and the little girl," Blaine clarified. "If you'd had the guts to go for the two of them, you could be happy right now."

"Who says I'm not?" he challenged them.

He had a great place in the city with a view of the lake, a fast car. The single lifestyle most married men would envy—most. Not these guys, but most. Maybe…

Ash laughed at him. "I know happy. And you're not it, my friend. You're miserable."

He couldn't argue with him. The new husband radiated happiness like a neon sign—making Dalton want to hurl…something. But they were at his condo, and he liked to keep the place neat, the way his grandmother had taught him.

"You guys don't know what you're talking about," he insisted.

He had seen Elizabeth's face when she'd realized it was her fiancé moving around on the floor—that he wasn't dead. She had been more than relieved; she had been elated. And since the nanny had arrived to care for Lizzie, she had ridden along in the ambulance with him and Jared Bell to the hospital.

"I never had a chance with Elizabeth," he told them.

"If you think that, you really are a damn fool," Blaine said. "That woman's in love with you."

"That woman was grateful," he said. "I found her in the trunk of that car when she was barely clinging to life, when she didn't even know who she was."

But she knew now. She was Tom Wilson's fiancée.

"Her memory didn't affect her feelings," Blaine said.

No. Seeing Tom Wilson nearly die had affected her, though. She loved the man. She wouldn't have been wearing his ring if she hadn't.

He shrugged. "I'm not going to argue this with you guys. The case is over."

Gregory Cunningham was dead. Kenneth and Patricia Cunningham's deaths had been ruled homicides. Just homicides. Their names were cleared because of Elizabeth, because she had been so determined that their memories be untainted for their daughter.

"The case is over," Blaine agreed.

"But you two don't have to be," Ash added.

Of course the happily married men would

think that. Who were the fools? They had just been damn lucky that the women for whom they'd fallen had loved them back.

Dalton had never been that lucky. "She's going to marry Tom Wilson." He was certain of that.

"Not if you stop the wedding," Blaine suggested.

Could he? Could he put his heart on the line without knowing if she even returned his feelings?

He'd already been accused of being a fool. What did it matter if he made one of himself? He would rather regret making a scene than never telling her how much he loved her. He should have told her before. He should have told her when they'd made love how much she meant to him. How he had never cared for anyone the way he cared for her.

"I really hate you guys," he muttered, even as he dug his car keys from the pocket of his jeans. They had goaded him into embarrassing himself. "You're enjoying this—enjoying that I'm going to make a fool of myself."

Why would Elizabeth choose him—an FBI agent with a penchant for danger—over the conservative lawyer she had already agreed to marry?

Blaine chuckled. "You've got it bad, Reyes. You're not your usual cocky self."

He wasn't—because he wasn't sure of Elizabeth's feelings. He was sure of his, though, and he would regret never sharing those feelings with her.

Even if she rejected him…

Ash just laughed and patted his back, urging him, "Go get your bride!"

REGRET PULLED THE fake smile from Elizabeth's face. She shouldn't have stopped by Tom's hospital room. But she had already been at the hospital visiting Agent Jared Bell. So she had stopped in out of courtesy.

Nothing more.

"As soon as I'm released, we should move in together," Tom was saying. He had already reached out for her hand and tugged her down onto the hospital bed next to him.

"What?" she asked. Clearly he must have sustained some brain damage from the gunshot wound to his head.

"You and the little girl can move into my condo in Chicago," he said as if extending a magnanimous offer.

She shook her head.

"It makes the most sense," he said. "It's bigger than your place. And really, you can't stay *here*."

"I can't?"

He chuckled. "Your job is in Chicago. Your life is in Chicago."

The love of her life was in Chicago. He must have been because she hadn't seen him since she had ridden away in the ambulance. She'd expected to see him at the hospital. That night. And maybe today.

That was one of the reasons she had come by to visit Jared Bell. She had been worried about him, too, though. It hadn't been all about Dalton.

"Lizzie's home is here."

"Lizzie is a child," he said. "She'll adjust."

"She only recently lost her parents." She sighed. "And now her uncle…" Gregory Cunningham had always been part of the child's life. The boogeyman. But she might miss him, too. "She's had a lot of adjustments to make."

"Exactly," he said. "She'll be fine. She has you."

"What about you?" she asked, wondering why he had stopped suggesting that she give up the child.

"I understand why you want to keep her."

He made Lizzie sound like a stray to whom she'd gotten attached.

"Why do you?" she asked. Did he have any feelings for the little girl? He had never paid any attention to her.

"To keep you," he said. "I would do anything to make you happy, Elizabeth."

Something cold and hard slid over her finger.

Her skin chilled and she shivered with revulsion. He'd put that damn ring back on her finger. "Tom…"

"Sorry," a deep voice murmured from the doorway. "I didn't mean to interrupt…"

She jerked away from Tom and turned toward the door—just in time to see Dalton's broad back as he walked away.

"Wait!" she called out to him, her heart beating quickly. "Dalton!"

Tom sighed. "I guess I have my answer."

"I didn't realize you'd asked me a question," she said as she tugged off the diamond. "You just assumed."

"You rode in the ambulance with me," he reminded her. "You acted like you cared—like you still have feelings for me."

"We were together a long time," she said. "I have feelings for you. But I don't love you."

"No," he agreed. "I see that now. I see who you love."

She hoped it wasn't too late to make Dalton see that she loved him. Would he care? Did he return her feelings? Her pulse raced.

"I'm sorry." As she passed his ring back to him, he caught her hand and held on to her.

"I feel sorry for you," he said, "because he's going to break your heart. He's not looking to be a husband or a father."

Maybe Tom was right. But that didn't stop Elizabeth. She tugged her hand free of his grasp and hurried into the hall. But Dalton was gone. She should have run faster.

She sucked in a sharp breath along with her disappointment.

"So when's the wedding?" a deep voice asked.

She glanced up and found him standing across the hall, in the doorway of an empty room. She shook her head and lifted her bare hand. "I'm not getting married."

Because Tom was probably right about Dalton. He had made his feelings clear about marriage and fatherhood before. He had no interest in them. The only thing he hadn't made clear to her was his feelings for her.

"Really?" he asked with a dark brow arched in skepticism. He leaned closer and studied her hand. "I swear I saw a ring on there just a second ago."

"Tom got the wrong idea," she said.

Dalton shrugged. "Can't say I blame him. You were awfully worried about him back at the house."

"I thought he was dead," she said. "I was relieved that he wasn't. Enough people had already died because of me."

"Because of Gregory Cunningham," he corrected her. "Not because of you. Nothing was your fault."

Guilt weighed so heavily on her as she admitted, "I told Kenneth to cut off Gregory."

"And you don't think he would have done that without your advice?" he asked. "From everything you told me about the guy, Kenneth Cunningham was smart. He wouldn't have kept giving his brother money."

She released a shaky breath and along with it, a lot of the guilt she'd been feeling. "No, he wouldn't have."

"But giving Wilson the wrong idea, that is your fault," he said. "If you hang out in his hospital room, he's going to think he has a chance."

"I didn't come here to see him," she said.

"Who did you come to see?" Dalton asked.

"Agent Bell," she replied. "I was relieved to see that he's doing well." So well that the profiler was being released later that afternoon—or so he'd told her.

"Jared said you'd been by his room."

She drew in a deep breath, swallowed her pride and admitted, "I was hoping that you would be here visiting him. I was really hoping to run into you."

His dark eyes brightened. "Seriously?"

She glanced uneasily back at Tom's room. This wasn't a conversation she wanted her ex-fiancé to overhear; she wasn't cruel.

"Do you want to come back to the house?" she asked. "And see Lizzie?"

His eyes brightened even more and a smile

curved his sensuous mouth. "I would love to see Lizzie."

As they headed down the hospital hall, he took her hand in his—the way he had so many times before. And as they stepped inside the empty elevator, he said, "But I really came here to see you."

Hope fluttered in her heart, lifting it.

ELIZABETH'S FACE FLUSHED with color at her embarrassment over finding the nursery empty. Dalton barely held back a chuckle at her reaction.

"I'm sorry," Elizabeth said as she read the note the nanny had left for her. "I didn't know Marta was taking Lizzie to a playdate with her grandchildren."

"I did," Dalton admitted.

Her eyes widened in surprised. "How?"

"I suggested it when I came here earlier."

"You were here earlier?" she asked, her beautiful eyes widened in surprise. "Why?"

"I played with Lizzie," he said, and his grin slipped out now with the memory of how happy the little girl had been to see him. She'd clung to him. And he'd been so happy to hold her and play with her. "I missed her."

She nodded. "She's such a special little girl."

"Yes, she is," he wholeheartedly agreed. "You're lucky to have her."

She blinked her thick lashes as if fighting back tears. "Yes, I am."

"And she's lucky to have you," he said. "You're very special, too, Elizabeth."

She smiled, but there was a tinge of sadness to it. And she continued to blink furiously, as if she was about to cry.

"What's wrong?" he asked. He hoped she didn't still feel guilty about becoming little Lizzie's guardian.

"I just realized what this is," she said with a quick gesture at his chest.

"What is this?" he asked.

"Goodbye."

When he'd found her in Tom Wilson's room—in what had looked like an intimate moment—he'd thought he might have been too late. But then she had called out to him. And she'd come out of that room without the ring on her finger. Hope warmed his heart—along with all the love and passion he felt for her.

He slid his arms around her and pulled her close. Then he covered her mouth with his. He'd missed the sweet sigh of her breath as she kissed him back. He'd missed her lips and the way she ran her fingers into his hair and clutched him closer. When he could lift his mouth from hers, he asked, "Does that feel like goodbye?"

She shook her head.

He swung her up in his arms and carried her down the hall to that sunshine-filled master bedroom. He undressed her slowly, kissing every inch of silky skin as he exposed it to his sight and his touch.

She moaned and sighed, reacting to his every caress—his every kiss. He made love to her thoroughly and, most of all, lovingly—making sure that she had no doubt about his feelings.

But yet he didn't utter the words that burned in his throat. He wasn't sure how to say something he'd never said before. So, after shouting his release, he collapsed back on the bed, and he fell silent.

She lay on his chest, panting for breath. Once she'd regained it, she pulled away from him. "I'm sorry," she said. "You probably need to go back to the hospital."

He pressed a hand over his madly beating heart. "I'm fine," he said. "I don't need medical attention." He needed her attention, but she wouldn't look at him.

"I meant that you probably have to pick up Agent Bell," she said. "I know he's being released this afternoon."

He nodded. "Yeah, he is," he said, "probably against medical orders."

"Why would he leave, then?"

"A young woman recently disappeared," he said

with a shudder as he remembered how Elizabeth
had nearly disappeared forever.

If he hadn't stopped that car…

"That's awful," she murmured with a shiver
of her own.

He wrapped his arms around her for comfort and warmth and to pull her closer. "Yes," he
agreed. "Jared thinks it could be related to his
case."

"Do you?"

He shrugged. "I don't know."

He actually thought Jared Bell was a lot like
Captain Ahab, and that he was going to kill himself trying to catch the elusive serial killer.

"I guess it's a good thing that I'm not getting
married, then," she said.

"Why would you say that?" he asked. He was
glad she wasn't marrying Tom Wilson. But did
she have no intention of ever getting married?

"I don't have to worry about that serial killer."

"No, you don't," Dalton said, "because you have
me to protect you."

"I do?" she asked. And finally she looked at
him again, staring up at him with her silvery-gray
eyes wide and hopeful.

"This isn't goodbye." He reached for the bedside table where he'd left his holster and gun. But
that wasn't all he'd left there. Beneath the holster,

he'd hidden a small jewelry case. It wasn't as big a diamond as Tom Wilson had put on her hand.

But she gasped when he opened the case. And tears shimmered in her eyes. "What are you doing?"

"Proposing," he said. "I know I'm not doing a very good job of it, though. But I've never done this before. I've never even told anyone that I loved them."

"You haven't told me," she said. "But I haven't told you, either."

He tensed in anticipation of humiliation. Had he just made the fool of himself that he'd worried he would?

"But I do," she said. "I love you very much."

And finally the words poured from his lips. "I love you, Elizabeth Schroeder. I love your strength and your courage and your loyalty. I love everything about you."

"Even when I didn't know who I was," she said, "it was like you knew me."

"I do," he said. "I know how amazing you are. And how much I want you to be my wife." He thought fleetingly of that serial killer that was still eluding Jared Bell. "And I promise you that I won't let anything happen to my bride."

"I thought you would never take a bride," she murmured.

"I thought I would never, either," he admitted.

"Until I found you in that trunk. Ever since then you were destined to be my bride. Will you marry me?"

"It was destiny," she said, "that you found me. And every promise you've made to me, you've kept. I can't wait to be your bride and your wife."

His hand shook slightly as he slid the ring onto her finger. It fit perfectly—just like the two of them. "I can't wait to be your husband," he said, "and Lizzie's father."

Tears filled her eyes again and spilled over to trail down her beautiful face. He brushed them away with his thumbs. "Don't cry."

"These are happy tears," she assured him. "Kenneth and Patricia would be so happy for us—for all of us."

"We can stay in this house," he said.

"Our jobs are in Chicago," she said. "And wherever we are will be Lizzie's home. Our home."

"We can have two homes," he said. "One in the city and one here. I will do whatever necessary to make you and our little girl happy."

"You already have," she said. "I love you."

She was right. It didn't matter where they lived. It only mattered that they were together—the three of them and the additional children he knew they would have someday.

"I love you," he said. "And I can't wait to marry you."

"I can't wait to marry you."

"I only have one problem," he said with a sudden and sickening realization.

"What problem?" she asked.

"My problem is that I don't know who to ask to be my best man," he replied.

She laughed. "That is a problem."

He laughed, too, as happiness overwhelmed him. He had never realized how much he could love someone—until he'd fallen for her and Lizzie. He didn't really care who his best man was. He only cared that she would become his bride. "Marry me," he said again.

She nodded and eagerly agreed, "As soon as we can get a license."

"There's a cute little church not far from here," he said. "I think you'll love it."

"I love you," she said. "It doesn't matter where we get married or where we live—as long as we're together."

"Forever," he vowed.

They had that same kind of love her friends had had—the forever-and-after, eternal love. Every promise they made each other would be kept.

* * * * *

LARGER-PRINT
BOOKS!

HARLEQUIN

Presents®

GET 2 FREE LARGER-PRINT
NOVELS PLUS 2 FREE GIFTS!

YES! Please send me 2 FREE LARGER-PRINT Harlequin Presents® novels and my 2 FREE gifts (gifts are worth about $10). After receiving them, if I don't wish to receive any more books, I can return the shipping statement marked "cancel." If I don't cancel, I will receive 6 brand-new novels every month and be billed just $5.30 per book in the U.S. or $5.74 per book in Canada. That's a saving of at least 12% off the cover price! It's quite a bargain! Shipping and handling is just 50¢ per book in the U.S. and 75¢ per book in Canada.* I understand that accepting the 2 free books and gifts places me under no obligation to buy anything. I can always return a shipment and cancel at any time. Even if I never buy another book, the two free books and gifts are mine to keep forever.

176/376 HDN GHVY

Name	(PLEASE PRINT)	

Address		Apt. #

City	State/Prov.	Zip/Postal Code

Signature (if under 18, a parent or guardian must sign)

Mail to the **Reader Service:**
IN U.S.A.: P.O. Box 1867, Buffalo, NY 14240-1867
IN CANADA: P.O. Box 609, Fort Erie, Ontario L2A 5X3

**Are you a subscriber to Harlequin Presents® books
and want to receive the larger-print edition?
Call 1-800-873-8635 today or visit us at www.ReaderService.com.**

* Terms and prices subject to change without notice. Prices do not include applicable taxes. Sales tax applicable in N.Y. Canadian residents will be charged applicable taxes. Offer not valid in Quebec. This offer is limited to one order per household. Not valid for current subscribers to Harlequin Presents Larger-Print books. All orders subject to credit approval. Credit or debit balances in a customer's account(s) may be offset by any other outstanding balance owed by or to the customer. Please allow 4 to 6 weeks for delivery. Offer available while quantities last.

Your Privacy—The Reader Service is committed to protecting your privacy. Our Privacy Policy is available online at www.ReaderService.com or upon request from the Reader Service.

We make a portion of our mailing list available to reputable third parties that offer products we believe may interest you. If you prefer that we not exchange your name with third parties, or if you wish to clarify or modify your communication preferences, please visit us at www.ReaderService.com/consumerschoice or write to us at Reader Service Preference Service, P.O. Box 9062, Buffalo, NY 14240-9062. Include your complete name and address.

HPLP15

LARGER-PRINT BOOKS!

GET 2 FREE LARGER-PRINT NOVELS PLUS
2 FREE GIFTS!

♥HARLEQUIN®

Romance

From the Heart, For the Heart

YES! Please send me 2 FREE LARGER-PRINT Harlequin® Romance novels and my 2 FREE gifts (gifts are worth about $10). After receiving them, if I don't wish to receive any more books, I can return the shipping statement marked "cancel." If I don't cancel, I will receive 4 brand-new novels every month and be billed just $5.09 per book in the U.S. or $5.49 per book in Canada. That's a savings of at least 15% off the cover price! It's quite a bargain! Shipping and handling is just 50¢ per book in the U.S. and 75¢ per book in Canada.* I understand that accepting the 2 free books and gifts places me under no obligation to buy anything. I can always return a shipment and cancel at any time. Even if I never buy another book, the two free books and gifts are mine to keep forever.

119/319 HDN GHWC

Name	(PLEASE PRINT)	
Address		Apt. #
City	State/Prov.	Zip/Postal Code

Signature (if under 18, a parent or guardian must sign)

Mail to the **Reader Service:**
IN U.S.A.: P.O. Box 1867, Buffalo, NY 14240-1867
IN CANADA: P.O. Box 609, Fort Erie, Ontario L2A 5X3
Want to try two free books from another line?
Call 1-800-873-8635 or visit www.ReaderService.com.

* Terms and prices subject to change without notice. Prices do not include applicable taxes. Sales tax applicable in N.Y. Canadian residents will be charged applicable taxes. Offer not valid in Quebec. This offer is limited to one order per household. Not valid for current subscribers to Harlequin Romance Larger-Print books. All orders subject to credit approval. Credit or debit balances in a customer's account(s) may be offset by any other outstanding balance owed by or to the customer. Please allow 4 to 6 weeks for delivery. Offer available while quantities last.

Your Privacy—The Reader Service is committed to protecting your privacy. Our Privacy Policy is available online at www.ReaderService.com or upon request from the Reader Service.

We make a portion of our mailing list available to reputable third parties that offer products we believe may interest you. If you prefer that we not exchange your name with third parties, or if you wish to clarify or modify your communication preferences, please visit us at www.ReaderService.com/consumerschoice or write to us at Reader Service Preference Service, P.O. Box 9062, Buffalo, NY 14240-9062. Include your complete name and address.

HRLP15

LARGER-PRINT BOOKS!
GET 2 FREE LARGER-PRINT NOVELS PLUS
2 FREE GIFTS!

◆ HARLEQUIN

super romance®

More Story...More Romance